A SIXER OF TEQUILA

An Althea Rose Novel

TRICIA O'MALLEY

Lovewrite Publishing

A SIXER OF TEQUILA

Stand tall, darling…

Chapter One

"THE FLAMINGO'S BEEN STOLEN."

I leaned back on my stool and unabashedly eavesdropped on the women gossiping next to me under the thatched roof of Lucky's Tiki Bar, run by my best friend Beau. He winked at me from where he was building a mai-tai in one of the tiki mugs from his new custom line of mugs – this one in a shark shape – and I knew he was listening in as well.

"Can you believe it? Who would steal a six-foot-tall flamingo?" Woman number one, in a floral dress and tasteful flats, shook her head sadly as if to say *What is the world coming to?*

I, too, wondered what this world was coming to, but more because I was concerned over the taste of someone who would actually order a six-foot-tall flamingo. Granted, I shouldn't be passing judgment on other people's design tastes, as mine ran to the decidedly more eclectic side of things.

"They say it was going to be at the entrance for the new mini-golf course. They were going to unveil it and surprise the town this week." Woman number two, dark circles under her eyes and hair in an unkempt ponytail, shrugged. "Which is too bad. I've been telling the kids I had a surprise for them. At the very least, it would have been something to wear off some of their incessant energy."

That explained the dark circles and messy hair, I thought, and sipped delicately on my mojito as I considered the news. Tuning them out as they began to discuss their kids – a topic that could often send me straight to sleep – I wondered what had happened to the flamingo.

"Think it's just teens having a prank?" Beau came and leaned forward on the bar, his golden good looks and air of confidence making both men and women alike fall for him on the regular. But he only played for one team – and too bad it wasn't mine, I thought, once again admiring his handsome face and easy surfer style.

"Doesn't feel that way to me," I said. "But I also didn't know we were getting a mini golf course, so there's that."

"Didn't you? It's been the talk of the town for weeks now," Beau said with a smile. "Everyone's complaining about the name."

"No! I hadn't heard," I admitted, leaning closer. "Is it bad?"

"Flocking Flamazing Mini-Golf," Beau said, his eyes crinkling at the corners as he did his best not to laugh.

"Shut up. That's amazing," I breathed, immediately wondering what the Whittiers, Tequila Key's upper-crust family, would have to say about that. Frankly, I was surprised Theodore Whittier hadn't stopped the development in its tracks already. He was on the board of everything in town, as he liked to tell anyone who cared to listen.

I never did.

"Don't you mean *fla*-mazing?" Beau asked. I laughed out loud this time while Beau went off to serve some tourists who had just arrived at the end of the bar.

Tequila Key was just a bump on the road on the way to the party town of Key West. I liked the sleepiness of the town, where everyone knew everyone and something as small as a new mini-golf course was enough to send the town into full gossip mode. Years ago, some intrepid mayor had decided to put a sign on the highway proclaiming, "Tequila Makes it Better," thus ensuring that no tourists would ever actually visit Tequila Key. Instead they just stopped to take a ridiculous selfie by the sign before continuing on their way. I was more than happy with this arrangement, though I'd heard murmurs lately about a new town campaign seeking to encourage more tourism. Personally, after the last few months I'd had, more tourists were the last thing I was looking for. My name had been splashed across the tabloids more than once, and I was finally settling back into a normal routine with nobody hounding me for psychic information.

Aside from my clients, that is.

I'm Althea Rose, co-owner of the Luna Rose Potions & Tarot Shop. I was recently outed to the world as a psychic by several gossip magazines and a reality show producer – whom I'd subsequently helped put in jail – and my client list has exploded ever since. Granted, I shouldn't say I'd been 'outed' – I'd never hidden the fact of who or what I was – but I certainly didn't enjoy looking at my life through the lens of a tabloid magazine. Not to mention that the editors liked to choose the most unflattering photos of me they could find. It was enough to put anyone off wearing a swim-suit in public ever again.

"Did you hear about the flamingo?" Luna, my other best friend and colleague, slid onto a stool next to me, looking imminently cool and perfectly put-together in her white linen maxi-dress, not a wrinkle in sight. I mean, how was that even fair? Not only was she coolly gorgeous with flowing blond hair, twinkling blue eyes, and a smile that could drop men to their knees, but even her linen dresses didn't crease. I suspected, as I had on more than one occasion, that she used a glamour spell to keep her whites white and her clothes unwrinkled.

There were some extra benefits to being a white witch, I supposed.

"Apparently that's the gossip of the hour," I said. I

nodded to the two women who were walking out the door, presumably to attend to their aforementioned children, and turned to look back at Luna. "How did I not even know there's going to be a mini-golf course going in?"

"You've been pretty tied up. Between the deluge in clients and your new love life, I'm surprised you've even had time to come up for air," Luna said, nodding to Beau when he held up a bottle of pinot grigio.

"It's not a love life," I protested, squirming in my seat.

"Fine, sex life. Whatever you want to call it." Luna blew out an exasperated breath – well, as close to exasperated as she gets with me – and gratefully accepted the glass of wine Beau handed her.

"Oh, are we talking about sex? Whose sex life?" Beau said, leaning in, his eyes dancing in curiosity.

"Althea's." Luna gestured to me with her wine glass. "I'm just pointing out that she's doing the thing she always does when she first starts dating someone and disappears off the radar for a while. Which is how she didn't know about the mini-golf course, let alone the stolen flamingo."

"Well, in all fairness, the flamingo bit is a new twist," Beau said, ever my champion. "But yeah, she's totally doing her hermit thing. We're just her friends when she's not having sex."

So much for being my champion.

"That's not true!" I tugged a lock of my hair, dyed

blue this month, and glared at them. "You all know how nutso my life was after the tabloids. I could barely go outside after we were involved with that reality show producer. And, well, yes, I like sex. So sue me. It's good stress relief."

"You'd think she'd be less bitchy with all the sex she's getting," Luna pointed out.

"Right? Like, where is the relaxed Althea we all know and love?"

"I'm right here," I pouted as I took another sip of my mojito.

"See? That's the face you'd think she wouldn't be making after all the sex she's having."

"I'm not cranky," I insisted. "I just don't like you insinuating that I drop my friends as soon as I'm dating someone."

"You don't drop us, you just take a small holiday," Luna amended, carefully brushing away a small speck of dust on the bar that had dared to get close to her dress.

"Doesn't everyone, though? I seem to remember you disappearing for a significant amount of time once you and Mathias hooked up." Luna had the decency to look away and hum. "And you, Beau – I know the minute you're hooking up because you start buying new clothes."

"Date outfits," Beau agreed.

"Well? I'm here, aren't I? When I could be home

shagging a sexy dive instructor. So can we all appreciate that?"

"Appreciated." Luna ran her hand gently down my arm. "Now, who would steal a six-foot flamingo?"

"And why do I feel like you're about to get involved in it?" Beau said, glaring at me.

"Me?" I squeaked, pointing a finger at my chest. "I don't care about this stupid flamingo."

"But you love a mystery." Luna tucked a wisp of blonde hair behind her ear. "I don't have a great feeling about this, I'll be honest."

"It's just a flamingo. What harm could come from finding out who took a silly plastic statue? As Beau said, it's probably just teens playing a prank."

"I don't like flamingos," Luna said.

I gaped at her. "How can you not like flamingos? They're like..." I stopped, considering my words.

"The Beaus of the bird world? Though I think I'd prefer parrots, but parrots squawk way more than I do."

Both Luna and I suddenly found other things to look at in the restaurant.

"Ohhhh... aren't we both being bitchy today? I see how it is. Just for that, I'm going to make you a flamazing flamingle martini and you're going to love every drop of it."

"Flamingle?" Luna wondered out loud to Beau's retreating back.

"Trust me, you'll flocking love it."

Chapter Two

I WASN'T out looking for trouble, I told myself as I wandered my way home from Lucky's. I took the long way on my beach cruiser, pulling to a stop in front of a shotgun style house. The worn porch wrapping its front was set several steps higher than the street. I peered into the dark corner, and jumped when someone tapped my arm.

"You're looking a little stalkerish." Miss Elva – our resident voodoo priestess, among many other magickal gifts – stood resplendent before me in a screaming orange caftan and a bedazzled blue hair wrap.

"Jeeeeezus," I proclaimed, holding my hand to my heart. "You'll give a girl a heart attack, sneaking up on me like that."

"No wonder you always getting in trouble, child, if you can't even hear me calling your name from halfway down the block."

"Were you really? Huh, maybe I am really distracted today. Or tired. Either way, yes, I was looking for you. Where are you coming from?"

"Oh, now she wants to know my business. See? She *is* stalking me." Miss Elva shook her head sadly.

"She was out meeting a man," said Rafe, Miss Elva's pirate ghost. He trembled in rage over her shoulder. Sniffing, he looked down his nose at me. "Not that you'd know what that was like, what with the outfits you wear and all."

"What's wrong with my outfits?" I looked down at my flowy maxi-dress, which I considered to be my uniform in the unrelenting heat of Tequila Key.

"Don't mind him, honey. He's just in a tizzy because Miss Elva was out flirting with a real man." Rosita, a new addition to Miss Elva's ghostly pack, materialized next to her shoulder, studying her nails as Rafe shot her a glare.

"Like you can call that puffed-up orange glazed doughnut of a thing a man," Rafe scoffed, then shut his mouth at Miss Elva's look.

"Now, you know how I feel about fat-shaming, Rafe. The man may have a little extra to love on him, but that doesn't mean he's a doughnut," Miss Elva said.

"I wasn't fat-shaming. You people seem to love your doughnuts," Rafe argued back, trailing behind Miss Elva as she climbed her porch. She settled into her corner rocking chair and waved for me to join her. I eyed Miss Elva's straight wood-backed visitor's chair –

with no cushion, mind you – and decided to stand instead. Leaning against the railing, I nodded to Rosita.

"How's things, Rosita? You settling into this new world?"

"I'm good, Althea. At least someone has the manners to ask about me once in a while."

I refrained from pointing out that since Luna, Miss Elva, and I were the only ones who could see her, it wasn't likely that anyone else would step up and ask how she was doing.

"Glad to hear it. I know it was an adjustment when you joined us." 'Adjustment' might be a slight under-statement since, much like Rafe, she'd popped through the veil during a spell. To Rafe's horror and my never-ending delight, Rosita had been a brothel owner during Rafe's time on earth and knew all about his exploits. Or lack thereof, I should say. As pirates and plundering went, it seemed the ladies of the night at Rosita's estab-lishment were often left unplundered when it came to Rafe.

"I love it here. Women own businesses without being harassed like I was, and there's so much tech-nology we never had. I have to say, this has been not only an education, but a load of fun. I definitely plan to stay around."

Rafe groaned and shook his head.

"Now you just let her be, Rafe. She deserves a second chance at experiencing this world, just like you have."

"I know, my lovemountain. But can't she go experience it over there? Like way over there. Why does she have to be with us all the time?"

"I can go home with Althea if that's what you want." Rosita crossed her arms and glared at Rafe.

"I'd like nothing more," Rafe said, beaming.

"Wait a minute…" I protested.

"Fine, then I'll go hang out with her for a while. But you remember when you're bored and crying over Miss Elva finding herself a real man that you'll have nobody to talk to. Don't come crying my way that there's another woman you can't satisfy," Rosita sniffed.

Dang, these ghosts were cold-hearted, I thought, and then gave myself a little mental slap. Of course they were cold-hearted. They no longer had hearts.

"Children," Miss Elva said, making a swooshing motion with her hand and then setting her rocker to rocking. "Enough with the bickering. Let's see what Althea was doing snooping around the porch."

There was a bit of sting to her words. We'd gone through a rough patch as of late and were still a little prickly with each other. But, as with most of the friends in my life, Miss Elva wasn't going anywhere, and neither was I. We'd been through too much together to give up on each other so easily.

"I wasn't snooping. I was stopping by to see someone who, in the past, was usually happy when I popped by for a visit."

Both Rosita and Rafe clamped their mouths shut and looked to Miss Elva to see what she would do.

"I'm sorry, child. That I am. I have a headache today." Miss Elva pinched her nose and rocked in her chair. "This heat is making me crankier than usual. Or there's something stirring in the air. I haven't bothered to look ahead yet. I'm still recovering from all the past drama."

"How are sales on your trucker hats?" Miss Elva had exploded into the national spotlight when the tabloids had come through. While the tabloids had been mean to me, they loved her, and she'd been an instant sensation. Capitalizing on the fame, she'd made up some merchandise to sell. You couldn't call the woman stupid, that's for sure. She'd made a fortune.

"Incredible. We've expanded to my own designer caftan line now. Who knew I'd be the head of a fashion house?"

"I'm not surprised. You always look fantastic." I wasn't lying, either. Miss Elva could pull off glitter, sequins, and feathers better than any burlesque dancer on stage. She never looked silly either; it just fit her style so well.

"Don't I know it. But thank you. I've been able to get my ideas into production, and I even have a website now. Want to see it?"

"I'd love to."

Miss Elva slid a slim tablet from her purse and

tapped the screen, swiveling it in her lap so I could look at the website she pulled up.

ELVA. Her name – first name only, mind you – was affixed to the top of the website in stark black against a white backdrop. Below, the website exploded into color as a river of shimmering crystals moved across the screen before dripping into images of caftans available for sale. Each caftan was starkly different and beautifully rendered, and there was enough variety that even the most conservative of people could comfortably test the waters with Miss Elva's designs. In short, she'd done a fantastic job.

"Miss Elva, I'm speechless! You're an honest-to-goddess fashion designer. These are so beautifully done. I can already see a few I'd want. You know, I was expecting more flash and… I don't know, I guess, wild designs from you. But these are you, just toned down a bit. Like…you, but translated for others."

"That's exactly it, honey. I know not everyone has the oomph that I do to pull off my looks, you get what I'm saying? I told that designer he'd better show me watered-down designs of me, and then I sent him about a hundred photos of my most favorite looks. And, well, he took it in stride and delivered. Though I did insist on a few that were just *me*. Because, come on, I can't be the only one fabulous enough to pull this off." Miss Elva clicked on a caftan image that exploded in sparkles, an intricate design of butterflies against a leafy green backdrop.

I had to agree – not everyone could pull it off. But everyone would wish they could.

"I'm really proud of you. I'll admit, I struggled with the trucker hats, as I thought you were being a little fame-hungry. But this? This is beautiful. You've really created something special here," I said, tapping the tablet.

"The trucker hats were just to help me get a down payment on these, child. You think I can't see the future? I knew the hats would be a flash in the pan, so I wanted to make money fast. But my designs? Well, these are my legacy. Elva is going to be a resort-wear brand that anyone who's anyone will know to buy. Trust me, this is going to be a hit."

"I don't doubt it. They are stunning. I'm really proud of you. You're going to be a smashing success with these! Are you happy with your designer? And the company producing them?"

"I am. I even went and met the people sewing the clothes. It's important to me that I see it from the ground up."

"When do you launch?"

"Two months or so. I can't wait."

"Everyone's going to see how amazing my love-mountain is," Rafe said, hovering by Miss Elva's shoulder.

"I think we already knew how wonderful she is." I straightened, squeezing her shoulder before resuming my post by the railing. "Now, who is the orange doughnut?"

"He's called the Flamingo King. Can you even believe it?" Rafe shot around the porch, warming to his favorite emotion – outrage. "What kind of self-respecting man calls himself the Flamingo King?"

"I... I'm at a loss, I'll admit."

"Oh, hush up, now. He *is* the Flamingo King. As in, he sells flamingos as his business."

"Live ones? Can you do that?"

"No, honey, like the one that was stolen today. He sells them to amusement parks, golf courses – anybody, really. In all sizes, shapes, and types – flamingo floaties, flamingo statues, flamingo yard ornaments. You name it, he's got it. Well, flamingo-themed, that is."

"Is that... well, is that profitable?"

"Child, sho is. He has himself a nice little island estate in the Bahamas and a massive yacht to sail on."

"Huh, who would've thunk it? So, I presume it's his stolen flamingo that's the gossip of the day?"

"So it seems."

"And what do we know about it?"

"Nothing at the moment. But I suspect we'll be finding out more as the days unfold. Speaking of, I made you something," Miss Elva fished in her purse and held up a small burlap bag wrapped in twine with a little blue bead attached.

"Oh shit. Why do you think I need gris-gris? No, I

don't want it." I stubbornly crossed my arms over my chest.

"Ungrateful wench," Rafe muttered.

"Silly woman," Rosita agreed.

"I think they've accurately summed up my thoughts," Miss Elva said, still holding up the gris-gris. Sighing, I reached out, took it, and tucked it in my pocket, feeling the thrum of power pulse from the small bag. "You know the rules. Keep it with you and all that. You remember what happened the last time you didn't."

"I remember, though I'd like to forget it." I shuddered at the memory of a fish eating Renaldo's eyeball on the dive where we had found his dead body. It was a scene that I wished I could erase from my brain, and had woken me up more than a time or two at night.

"You can't stop the rain, but you can bring an umbrella."

"So, you're saying a storm's coming?"

"Storm's a-comin' indeed, child. I'd warn Luna as well."

"On it."

Chapter Three

THE REST of the ride home from Miss Elva's was less than pleasant, though a lovely sunset painted the sky above me a stunning pink, and a light breeze cut the heat that had accumulated during the day. As usual, two pointy little ears poked over the windowsill of my house. Hank's internal radar apparently went off whenever I got within a block of home. No matter what time of day I came home, he somehow always seemed to know.

"Hey, buddy." I immediately bent over and pressed a kiss to Hank's smushface, and laughed as he bounded across the room. His little black and white body trembled in delight as he found today's toy – a stuffed shark – and came racing back across the room, skidding to a halt at my feet. Tugging the shark from his mouth, I launched it across the room and then sniffed the air.

Something smelled... well, delicious, and not like anything I'd be capable of concocting.

"Trace? Are you cooking?"

"That I am, lovely lady. I had a hankering for curry, plus I wanted to celebrate," Trace said, drying his hands on a towel and gesturing to me with the wooden spoon. All long and lanky, Trace looked at home in my kitchen. His hair was pulled back in a knot and his shirt loosely buttoned so that I could see the tangle of necklaces at his throat and a teasing of the tattoo that covered his chest.

"Mmm, this is delicious," I all but purred, beyond happy to have someone in my house cooking for me. That's the thing – I'm a woman of many talents. I'm a successful business owner, I can read tarot like a boss, and I can shoot some stunning underwater photography. But some of the more traditional womanly roles evaded my reach. I was a failure in the kitchen, I could rarely keep a plant alive, and housekeeping was best left to the lovely woman I hired to come in every two weeks to make sure I didn't end up dying in a pile of dust and dirty dishes.

"Mmm, that man is what's delicious. I'm surprised at you, Althea. I didn't think you had it in you to land a nice specimen like this one," Rosita practically panted in my ear, and I almost dropped the spoon back into the curry. Stiffening, I glared over my shoulder at her. Rosita just laughed, her dark curls bouncing along with her other considerable assets as she floated across the room to examine my space, Hank trailing behind her with a – dare I say – besotted look on his face. Whenever Rafe came to visit, Hank would do everything in his power to terrorize him, a behavior I particularly enjoyed. But this ghost? If I didn't know better, I'd say Hank was love-stricken.

"Is everything okay?" Trace asked, looking over his shoulder to see what I was staring at. I kept forgetting he couldn't see ghosts like I did. One reason I loved Trace was that he calmly accepted all the otherworldly things I was involved in, whereas certain past boyfriends of mine, not naming names – *Cash*, ahem – were a little more sensitive to the ol' ghosts and magick hoopla that I routinely surrounded myself with.

"Yup. Rosita's come to join us for a while," I explained, nodding to where Hank was mooning over a pink velvet chair in the corner. "Rafe's shot his mouth off one too many times and she's decided to visit over here. I suspect Rafe will grow bored and want her company after a bit, but for now, she's our new houseguest."

"Far out," Trace said, studying the corner where Hank had rolled on his back, his tongue lolling from his mouth. I shook my head sadly; I swear that dog had no shame.

"Hank, you don't just roll over for any lady who comes through the door. Have some decency, man," Trace called, mirroring my thoughts.

"Seriously, Hank. It's not that kind of party," I

added, and Hank rolled over and trotted toward us, convinced that since we were in the kitchen and speaking his name, food would inevitably follow.

"I like the furry one. He's charming," Rosita decided, perching on the chair.

"Trace or Hank?"

"Both, really. But it's nice to have a dog around who loves you without expectation of anything but love back. It's... a simple thing, but not something I would take for granted. Too many people had expectations of me in the past. To do so many things, to be a certain way, perform certain acts... it's nice with a dog. They just want to give and get love. So simple."

Her comments made me pause. I'd liked Rosita from the moment she'd popped through into our world; she had a biting wit, and a steel backbone which I could only imagine was honed from years of running a brothel in a time where women weren't supposed to be entrepreneurs. I hadn't stopped to ponder the more difficult or lonely aspects of her life, and I found myself warming to her more. Even though it meant that I essentially had a third wheel in my house for an undetermined amount of time.

"He is the gift that keeps on giving," I agreed, bending down and producing a treat for an ecstatic Hank. I smiled as, his expectations met for appropriate dog-to-human kitchen interactions, he bounded back across the room to Rosita.

"I don't see why Rafe hates him so. He's not a

beast," Rosita crooned. "Just the sweetest lovebug, isn't he?"

"It's likely because Hank chases Rafe around the room and barks like he's trying to kill him. The more Rafe races away, the more Hank gives chase. Rafe hasn't figured out yet that it's all a big game to Hank."

"I'd dearly love to see that particular spectacle."

"It's great. We'll get Miss Elva to come by soon, and Rafe will follow as he always does. You'll be in for a treat." I picked up a glass of red wine that Trace had poured for me, belatedly realizing that I was essentially standing in the kitchen talking to myself. Seeing the bemused expression on his face, I turned my attention to him.

"Sorry, I know I look crazy. Rosita can't understand why Rafe hates Hank."

"Because Hank reads people, or ghosts for that matter, really well." Trace smiled to the corner where Hank once again had rolled over on his back, and had a drugged look on his face as Rosita cooed over him.

"Anywho, back to you. Hi, how was your day, and just what are we celebrating?" I clinked my glass to his before leaning in for a lingering kiss. It was still a shock to my system that we'd moved from best friends to lovers, and I suspected Trace wanted more from me than that. For some reason, I wasn't ready to really put a label on things, though it was well-known in Tequila Key that we were partnered up. It was just… I seemed to have an actual phobia about taking things a step further. I figured if everything was good right now, why mess it up with big steps like commitment and sharing each other's space? I liked my space just fine. Sharing it certainly had its benefits, but alone time was precious to me. If I didn't recharge on a regular basis from the stress of reading for clients, I'd go mental before the year was out.

"We are celebrating a very lucrative job offer I just accepted."

"Wait… what? A job offer? I thought you liked your job." I wasn't sure if I was supposed to be happy or not, as I was so proud of Trace for having built his dive business and regular clientele from scratch.

"I love my job. I'm not leaving my job; I'm just expanding for a little while. I've been asked to join a luxury charter in the ABC islands, and I'll lead all the dives."

"For… like, a season? A week? What does this mean exactly?"

"This first one would be for three weeks. We'll do a week around each island. Half the group are divers and the other half aren't, so I'll lead the divers while the rest shop and explore. It's killer money, Althea, more than I could make on my own during those three weeks. Not to mention there's a likelihood of good tips if the customers like me."

"Of course they'll like you; everybody likes you." Except Cash, I thought, the name coming unbidden to my mind. Otherwise, what I spoke was truth. Trace was kind of like Beau – handsome, approachable, and could charm just about everyone who crossed his path. His easy likeability and extreme competence in diving made him a popular dive guide, and he was often booked up far in advance these days.

"Well, thank you, that's sweet of you. So, do you think I should take it?"

"You haven't said yes? Why not?"

"I wanted to talk it over with you. That's three weeks I'll be gone, potentially longer depending on the next gig."

"When would you leave?"

"In two days."

"Two days! That's crazy. How can anyone plan like that?"

"Apparently the other dive master got pneumonia and doesn't trust himself to go on a trip like that when he's still not fully recovered. And I had blocked my calendar off so I could do some repairs on the boat."

"Well… then I guess it's all meant to be. I'm excited for you!"

"Does it bother you that I'd be gone that long?" His blue eyes measured mine over my wine glass.

"No, of course not. I mean, I'll miss you, but we can still talk on Skype, right?"

"Of course. And three weeks isn't all that long anyway."

"Nope, and you know I love my alone time to

recharge my batteries. Hank and I will be just fine here by ourselves."

"And with me!" Rosita called from the corner, and I stifled a groan.

"What was that?" Trace asked, sliding his arms around me, pulling me close so that our bodies aligned. I could feel the heat of his skin through my dress.

"Rosita reminded me she'd be here for company."

Trace said nothing, only laughing into my mouth as he kissed me. He knew full well I'd be contemplating ways to banish Rosita from my house before the week was out.

Who could blame me? A woman needs her space.

Chapter Four

IT WAS a testament to my patience and my enjoyment of making a living from what I love to do that I didn't throttle my clients by the end of the day. It had been two days since word of the stolen flamingo had run rampant through Tequila Key, like a match thrown into a bushel of hay, and now it was the first thing anyone brought up for their small talk of the day.

Here's the thing about small towns – you can't just go about your day and quickly get anything accomplished. There's a slower pace and rhythm to small towns, and much of it has to do with making time for small talk so the word doesn't get out that you're a rude woman who hates people. Now, if I was to be totally honest, I didn't mind being labeled as such – I could be much more productive running my errands if everyone just steered clear of me – but alas, being a rude woman wasn't the best for business. So I pasted a smile on my face and bit my tongue during the inevitable small talk that greeted me at the pharmacy, the market, and always at a client appointment. I found that most clients were unable to walk into my office and just get down to business. Much like sex, it was in the best interests of us both to warm up a bit.

"A stolen flamingo? I just heard. Isn't that something?" I murmured to Melody, a new client who hung out with the pearl-clutchers in the fancier part of town. She had crossed the tracks, so to speak, to slum it up at my shop.

To be clear, the Luna Rose Potions & Tarot shop was my heart and I couldn't be prouder of the work Luna and I had put in to make our individual efforts shine. I was proud of my profession, and there was nothing more rewarding than helping people on a regular basis. But I'd be a liar if I said there wasn't a stigma or a stereotype that went with my job. And the manicured-lawn sweater-set-wearing set of Tequila Key certainly had their very vocal opinions of my profession. None of which stopped each and every one of them from scheduling a reading with me, mind you.

But I'd be out a of a job if I told people's secrets.

"I worry for my safety, you know," Melody said. She was faintly blond, rigidly conservative in a white button-down, slim khaki pants, and a loose sweater tied over her shoulders. A grimace dared to mar the Botox holding her face in suspension.

"I don't think you have to worry. Truly. It's likely just some teenagers having a laugh."

"But what's next? I mean... we've had a lot of drama for a small town lately. I wonder if we need to move somewhere safer." Melody cast a look at me, reminding me I'd been at the heart of much of the recent drama.

"I suspect any city has its crime, Melody. Surely there's no need to pack up and move because of a stolen flamingo."

"No... I suppose that would be rash," Melody laughed. At least I think she did; it was hard to tell with her face not moving.

"Is that what you'd like me to focus on for your reading today? Are you considering moving to a new place and wondering if it's the right path for you?" I handed Melody a stack of my favorite tarot cards – featuring Celtic fae illustrations – and she looked at them as though I'd handed her a tarantula.

"Shuffle the cards and think of your question," I prodded her gently.

She took a deep breath before nodding once. As she shuffled, I let my mental shields drop and let myself go into my zone, filtering out her thoughts and tuning into my inner guidance that helped me lead people on a healthy path.

"There, done," Melody said and placed the cards down on the table.

"Divide them into three piles, please."

After she had done that, I stacked the cards and looked at Melody.

"Your question?"

"Will I have a baby?" Her eyes were huge in her face, and I glimpsed the deep-rooted sorrow within.

I lowered my eyes for a moment to focus on the cards. That was the thing about my job: It constantly humbled me. Rich, poor, snotty, asshole, or kind – everyone who came to me was human and had the same basic needs. To be loved, to want children or a better career, or to feel safe in their environment. The questions varied, but the themes were much the same. We all longed for certain things to fulfill us. For Melody? It was to be a mother.

Focusing my energy, I began to lay out the cards, reading quite easily from her head that she'd suffered seven miscarriages. The stress it had placed on her marriage was threatening to shatter them. Now I had a new reason for the rigidity I had sensed in her – it was sheer stress.

I truly hoped that whatever I saw would bring her peace, but I never lied to my clients. Going in, I closed my eyes, ignoring my cards for a moment to just rely on my psychic intuition. To be honest, I was expecting the worst, so I was pleasantly surprised to see a much more relaxed and happy-looking Melody bouncing a chubby baby boy on her knee. She looked good, with some weight from her pregnancy on her and a real smile on her face. Turning to the cards, I read the spread while

Melody sat, fingers clutched tightly in her lap, her eyes sheened with tears.

"There," I said, pointing to the outcome card of my spread.

"A sun?" Melody peered at the card I had tapped.

"This is the outcome card of the spread. I'll read you the rest of your cards, but because I can see how much this means to you, I want you to know that the Sun card is a great outcome card for you. It means I do see you having a child in the future."

"Seriously? You can see that? You're not just saying that so I tip you?" Melody said, tears over spilling onto her cheeks, making tracks through her makeup.

"Yes, I can see that. Listen, I don't tell people what they want to hear. Sometimes I see spreads that look all rosy and good, then I come to the outcome card and it's bad. Which means life will throw you a curveball and you'll have to weather that storm. And I do not shield a client from that, because they should be prepared. But this spread? With this outcome card? Yes, I do see you having a very happy outcome." I reached over the table and squeezed her hand. "Be at peace, Melody. Your happiness is on its way."

"Thank you," she breathed, pulling a pressed cotton handkerchief from her purse. Who even used real handkerchiefs anymore? I briefly wondered. "I needed to hear this."

"I'm glad I could help," I said, and took the rest of the appointment to go over the rest of the card spread with her. As she left, after leaving a healthy tip, she paused at the door.

"Thank you again for your help, and for being kind with my grief. I don't know what everyone is talking about – you're not all that bad."

She was gone before I could respond, and I sat there with my mouth open. It was only when I heard Luna laughing at the door that I looked up.

"I swear to goddess, Luna, I try so hard with these people and they drop these bombs so casually, like I should be grateful for their approval."

"You did good there, Althea. Even if she didn't realize how bitchy she was being at the end."

"Thank goddess that's my last appointment for the day. I'm about done hearing about this stolen flamingo."

"When's her baby coming?"

"Not long now. A boy."

"I'll put together a little gift from our shop, just so she remembers who gave her hope." Luna, ever a nicer person than I, was already making a note in her planner.

My phone rang before I could respond, and I checked it to see Miss Elva on the display.

"Miss Elva," I answered, putting her on video so she could see Luna was in the shop with me as well.

"Hi, lovely ladies, how was your workday?" Miss Elva asked, her whole face filling the screen. She hadn't quite worked out the right distance to hold her phone at yet.

"Saving lives left and right," I grumbled.

"It was another great day," Luna amended, smiling over my shoulder at Miss Elva.

"Good. Althea, you can tell me about it over dinner. We're going out with David and his son."

"We?"

"Yes, we. Pick me up at seven. We're going to Beau's new place and Beau's promised us a nice table."

"Is Luna coming?"

"No, she has a boyfriend." Miss Elva rolled her eyes like I should know better.

"And I don't?"

"Oh, are we calling him your boyfriend now? Seems to me you've been holding him at arm's length on that for a while."

"I'm not... it's just..." I ran a hand through my hair and tugged a curl in frustration. "Listen, I'm involved with Trace, as you well know."

"Maybe, but you're less involved than Luna. Plus, everyone falls in love with Luna, so bringing her on a double date is pointless when she's in love with Mathias."

Luna chuckled softly over my shoulder but made no comment.

"Now, how do you think Trace would feel about me going out on a double date when he just left town?"

"I think there's either trust in a relationship or there isn't."

Hmpf.

"I don't think I'd be happy with him going on a

double date."

"Well, stop calling it a double date then. You're just my chaperone. I mean, I know I'm more than enough personality for two men, but if I want to really decide whether I like the Flamingo King, I need to focus my energies on him, get what I'm saying?"

"So why don't you leave the son at home?"

"Althea Rose, I am asking you for a favor. You gonna make me call this man up and tell him to leave his son at home when he's already nicely asked me out on a date? How rude would I be?"

I bit my tongue, considering for a moment how much I really did not want to go to this dinner, but also how Miss Elva and I had hit a rough patch lately. It was time for me to step up and be a good friend to her.

"Fine, I will chaperone you to dinner. I'll pick you up at seven."

"Perfect. Wear something flattering. Not that dress."

"I…" What was wrong with my dress? I looked down at my purple maxi with bright white lilies smattered across it. Looking back at the phone, I saw that Miss Elva had already disconnected.

Luna shrugged. "It does have a bit of an eighties vibe."

"What's wrong with the eighties? It's coming back in style," I called after Luna as she left my shop, pulling the screen closed behind her.

"Not if you've had it since the eighties," Luna called back.

Chapter Five

"NOT THAT ONE."

I was standing in front of my closet examining my collection of maxi-dresses. I suppose I had gotten in a bit of rut, as they were my go-to choice for living in humidity so thick it made you dream of moving to the arctic. Plus, people expected a tarot card reader to wear flowy caftans and robes and the like. I found that in my business, it was best to play to stereotypes. Years ago, I'd gotten in a tizzy about changing my shop to make it more elegant and soothing, like a fancy doctor's office. Clients hated it, and business had slowed. I quickly changed it back, decorating with a heavy nod to the psychic world – filling the space with draped velvets, tchotchkes and statues from all over, rows of books on the psychic realm, and even a fake skeleton in the corner, whose t-shirts I routinely changed. This month he was sporting a faded Grateful Dead t-shirt, a nod to my father and to my name. I still wasn't sure if I was named for the song or the actual rose bush.

"What's wrong with this one?" I demanded, turning to glare at Rosita. The dress in question was new, a brilliant deep blue with turquoise beading at the neckline.

"You need to showcase your assets if you want a man. You have considerable assets. Use them," Rosita shrugged, rolling her eyes as if it was obvious for even a simpleton like me. Hank rolled over on the bed, smiling his doggy-drool smile up at Rosita. She floated over him, cooing away.

"My assets, as you say, are already being showcased. To one man. Trace. You met him, remember?" I pulled the maxi-dress over my head anyway, because I liked it and it made me feel good. Which was more than enough to wear on a non-date where I wasn't interested in luring a man.

"Yes, he is very attractive. But you don't claim him, so, I think maybe you want another man, yes?"

"I don't need another man, Rosita. One is enough."

"Is it? Shocking." Rosita looked genuinely stunned and I had to remind myself of the life she had lived.

"For me, yes. I don't have time to juggle more than one man, Rosita."

"You don't juggle them, you use them at the same time," Rosita, ever so helpful, explained as she drifted after me to the bedroom.

"I…" Stopping to consider the idea while I put mascara on, I realized I couldn't fault her wisdom. "Yes,

I suppose more than one man at once would be an efficient use of time management."

"See? You're learning."

"But for now, I'm happy with just the one, thank you."

"Your loss." Rosita followed me as I went downstairs and opened the door so Hank could have his nightly run-about before dinner.

"Are you coming to dinner or will you stay here?"

"Will Rafe be there?"

"I have no idea. He seems to get very angry when Miss Elva goes on dates, so I'm not sure he'll stick around to watch."

"Achhh, then, no. What's the point? I take great joy in seeing his feathers all ruffled. If he stays behind then I just sit and watch you look awkward."

"I am not awkward." I rounded the corner of my kitchen counter, knocking an apple from the fruit bowl in the process. It bounced to the floor and rolled to a stop below Rosita.

"Right."

"Oh come on, that was an accident. Hank! Come in! Dinner!" An ecstatic Hank barreled through the door, startling Rosita and sending the apple spinning across the floor. He barely stopped before his face was in his food bowl, and his little bum danced as he wiggled his way through dinner, always delighted with his meal. I didn't blame him; I often found myself dancing in my seat when my dinner was served too. Good food should be celebrated.

"I like your photos." Rosita startled me from smiling down at Hank, lost in my thoughts. Turning, I found her flitting around the underwater photographs that lined my walls. "We didn't have photography like this in my time. It was only paintings and drawings. You've given me a way to see the underwater world. It's really beautiful."

Touched, I leaned against the counter and studied Rosita. For all of her sharp edges, she had a romantic's heart. Well, soul, I supposed. As she no longer had a heart.

"I guess I never thought about that, Rosita. Yes, I really love being underwater and taking photographs of what I see there. It's like an entirely different world. You can lose yourself in the beauty of what the ocean showcases."

"I'd like to see it sometime. Do you think you could take me?"

"I… honestly I have no idea, Rosita. Do you know if you can go underwater as a spirit? Have you tried? This is fascinating, now that I think about it. You don't have to breathe, so you wouldn't need tanks. I feel like you'd just be able to zip beneath the surface and see what's what."

"Likely, but I'm… Well, it's quite silly, really. But I'm scared." Rosita shrugged a shoulder and looked away, leaving my mouth gaping in shock for a second before I snapped it closed.

"Scared? After all you've seen and done? Even having been dead and in the spirit world? Why on earth would you be scared?"

"I don't know how to swim," Rosita admitted.

"But…" I wondered briefly if knowing how to swim even needed to translate into the spirit world since they could walk through walls and crazy shit like that. But then I reminded myself of something I had learned with clients a long time ago.

Feelings aren't rational.

Fear is fear, and if that was what she was afraid of, then I would be happy to help her.

"If I held your hand on a dive, would that help?" Again, no idea how I'd hold a ghost's hand, but hey – in for a penny, in for a pound.

"Yes, I think it would. Thank you, Althea. No matter what people say, you're a good sort," Rosita said as she drifted across the room to look at my photograph of eagle rays.

"Why do people keep saying that to me?" I looked down at Hank who grinned up at me, ever my champion, and I bent to give him a pat. Opening his drawer, I pulled out today's toy – a rubber duck – and launched it across the room where he chased it in delight.

"Ah, men and their toys." Rosita looked down at him in adoration. "Some things never change."

Chapter Six

"I SEE YOU IGNORED MY ADVICE," Miss Elva sniffed as she opened the door to my Mini coupe.

"What's wrong with this dress? Rosita didn't care for it either."

"It looks basic."

"You're saying I'm a basic bitch?" I raised an eyebrow at her, and Miss Elva just raised hers back at me. Though, in all fairness, I think anyone would look basic next to Miss Elva's resplendence. Tonight she'd pulled out a shimmery rose-gold caftan, and had woven a delicate, glittery crown of leaves through her hair. She looked like an Amazon warrior goddess, and me her lowly servant.

"Do I really need to say it?" Miss Elva sighed once more and gathered her skirt to sit in the front seat. Looking around, I spied no trace of Rafe.

"Well, when your line becomes available, I'll be

sure to purchase a few pieces so as not to embarrass you in public. Where's Rafe?"

"He refuses to come watch me philander with other men. Can you believe that? He needs to get his head on straight. I've made it very clear that I am an independent woman and though I do love my sweet Rafeboo, a woman needs the pleasures of the flesh, if you get what I'm saying."

"I get it, I get it," I said hurriedly, doing my best to pull my mind away from images of Miss Elva's flesh and – yup, too late. Sighing, I shook my head. "Rosita stayed at home as well. She only wanted to come if she could see Rafe in a snit."

"Those two… like children, I tell you."

"Tell me about this Flamingo King and son. I thought you'd only just met him."

"Well, I did, honeychild. On a dating app, of all things."

I stored that tidbit away to examine another day. I'd be lying if I said I didn't want to know what Miss Elva's dating app lineup looked like.

"I didn't know you were using dating apps."

"It's a new thing I'm trying. It's kind of fun, like ordering from the takeout menu."

Again, trying to keep images of Miss Elva and sex out of my head was proving fruitless.

"Okay, so you met this king on there? If he's the king, why is he on an app?"

"Well, love, I consider myself a queen and I'm on there. It's lonely at the top, don't you know."

It was hard to argue with that logic.

"Do I call him Flamingo King, or does he have a name?" I turned the car down Tequila Key's main drag, where tourist shops mashed together with our local hardware stores and coffeeshops.

"His name is David and his son is named Randall. They were here to bring some flamingos over for the mini-golf course."

"That seems like something they could have their delivery guys do, no?"

"I think they just wanted to get off-island. David says it's nice to live where he does, but he misses the convenience of shopping at certain stores, or even just trying out new restaurants."

I wanted to point out that Tequila Key wasn't exactly a bustling metropolis with huge stores like Costco or Target, but we'd arrived at the restaurant. Two men stood by the door, the Flamingo King and prince, I assumed, based on the older one's flaming pink shirt and orangey-tan skin.

"There they are! The one in the pink is David. Isn't he a doll? Okay, make nice at the table, Althea. I think I could have something serious with this one."

Love is blind, I reminded myself.

I found a lucky spot on the street not far from the restaurant. The men waited as we approached, and I took the time to size them both up. David, the tanned older gentleman, had a mile-wide grin on his face and no hair to speak of. He wore a rattan hat with a wide pink band, and his nicely pressed pants were dotted with tiny flamingos. None of those things should have worked together, but somehow he managed to pull it off. I was beginning to see his appeal for Miss Elva, who was equally as loud and original. It was like watching two parrots greet each other, both squawking in delight as the rest of us stood by, dazzled by the color show. Randall, the son, was a quietly muted version of his father in simple linen pants and the palest of pink button-downs, his brown hair slicked with gel. He smiled kindly at me.

"I think I can see the attraction," Randall whispered and despite myself, I laughed.

"I feel like I need to wear sunglasses," I admitted, holding out my hand to introduce myself. "I'm Althea, by the way."

"Randall. Nice to meet you. I know you were expecting a date, but I'll be honest with you – I am somewhat seeing someone, which I was clear with my father about."

"Phew, that makes my night much easier as I am also somewhat involved with someone," I smiled at him more broadly this time, feeling the tension ease from my shoulders.

"Even better. Then we'll have a nice evening chaperoning these two with no expectations other than friends," Randall said, then turned to introduce me to his father. Before I could respond I was engulfed in a flaming pink hug, and almost stumbled back from the exuberance of the Flamingo King.

"Althea! An honest delight it is to meet you, I tell you. Miss Elva speaks of you so highly," David boomed.

"Does she now?" I slid a glance over his shoulder to Miss Elva who merely looked away, pretending to examine a potted flower plant outside the restaurant.

"Of course she does. Says you're one of her best friends and a renowned psychic. I'm so happy to meet you." I caught Randall stiffening at the word 'psychic,' and felt my walls go up. Here we go, I thought, another skeptic. People always had a reaction to me one way or the other, something I should be used to by now.

"That's very kind of her. I'm honored to call Miss Elva my friend."

Miss Elva smiled at me over David's shoulder and I felt the knot loosen in my stomach. It seemed we were back to the norm, and if it meant a few dinners out with her new love interest, I was happy to be here. Even if I could tell Randall was less than enthused with my profession. I could only imagine what he would think of Miss Elva if she told him all the magick and voodoo she could perform. Wondering briefly if Miss Elva had enlightened these men as to her extra-special abilities, I followed them to the door of Beau's upscale restaurant.

"As you should be. She's an up-and-coming fashion designer. I've seen her stuff, and I have to tell you –

she's going to be the next big thing in resort wear. Trust me, I know a good business venture when I see it. And Elva here? Well, she's got the instincts. It's gonna be a hit, that it is."

Just a fashion designer? I raised an eyebrow at Miss Elva, our silent communication telling me everything I needed to know.

You didn't tell him about your other profession.

That's on a need-to-know basis.

You don't think your lover needs to know?

He only needs to know how to please me, child.

Enough of that, I thought, and closed that wave of communication.

Dinner just got a lot more interesting.

Chapter Seven

"SO, ladies, may I order for you or do you prefer to do the picking?" David asked. I suspected he liked to order for everyone. Unfortunately for him, I preferred to look at the seafood underwater when I was diving instead of eating it, so I had to choose carefully at Beau's seafood restaurant.

"I'm sorry, I have a limited number of options here. I'll go with the vegetarian pasta." I smiled at David and he beamed back at me, making me feel comfortable once again.

"No problem, lovie, I just like to ask. You get whatever you like best. Elva?"

I noticed he got a free pass on not addressing Miss Elva as *Miss* Elva, and wondered how he pulled that off. Then again, maybe I didn't really want to know.

"You go ahead and pick for me. I trust your judgment," Miss Elva positively purred as she closed her menu. I did my best not to give her side-eye.

"I'll have the scallops," Randall decided. He closed his menu and we all waited while David boomed out our order for the hovering waiter, and really for the whole restaurant to hear. This one did not move about his world softly.

I turned to Randall while David reached across the table to hold Miss Elva's hand, entertaining her with a story about flamingo-themed diapers. "Do you live on Eleuthera as well?" I asked.

"I do. I'm head of merchandising and operations for my dad's company, and we kind of have our own little estate on Eleuthera. I'm in and out of Miami frequently for meetings and to oversee production, but I love the quieter life on the island. It's a good contrast for me, and I get the best of both worlds."

"Miami night life when you want it, reading on the beach when you don't?"

"Pretty much. Have you been to Eleuthera?"

"I haven't. I've heard the diving is nice. The reefs are still intact, I'm told, unlike some of the bigger Bahamian islands?"

"The diving is excellent, yes. There's a famous drift dive on one side of the island; I highly recommend it if you dive."

"I do. Underwater photography is actually a hobby of mine that's kind of turned into a side gig for me. I sell my prints online. It's not extremely lucrative, but it's a nice outlet for my creativity."

"That's fantastic. I've never been good with a camera. If you're able to get half as good as whoever took these photos" – Randall gestured to the black and white photos on the wall of the restaurant – "maybe you'll make some good money someday."

I wondered if he knew he was being insulting, but decided to gently put him in his place.

"These are my prints."

"Is that so? I'm shocked!" Randall said, looking appropriately chagrined. Then, ever the gentleman, he added, "I'm sorry, I must have sounded like a complete ass there, didn't I? I shouldn't have assumed you weren't capable of producing art of this quality."

"It's fine. I have a tendency to downplay my work," I admitted, taking a sip of the mojito the waiter had slid in front of me.

"That she does," Miss Elva confirmed, leaning in to our conversation. "Did you hear that, David? These fine prints on the wall are done by Althea herself. Not only is she the best psychic tarot card reader this side of the Mississippi, but she's a damn good photographer."

I noticed the smile fade from Randall's face again after the word 'psychic,' but David boomed over my thoughts.

"That is fantastic. I tell you, Althea, I've got just the spot for a few of your prints. We just remodeled a wing of our house on the island. I'd like to buy a few of your prints for the wall. Big ones, like these. Can you come take a look and pick what works best?"

"Um… you want me to come to the Bahamas? For a few prints? Wouldn't it be easier for me to just send you some suggestions? You can see my images on my website."

"Naw, you should come. I know one thing and that's flamingos. The rest I leave up to professionals like my son or the decorators. You come on down and see the house, pick the prints. I trust you."

"I –"

Randall spoke up. "Why don't you invite them to the gala this weekend? Then they'd have a party and an excuse to look at the new space."

"Dang it, that's a fabulous idea. Want to come to my gala this weekend, ladies? It's a big 'un, let me tell you that. We pull out all the stops. This isn't just a down-home BBQ in the Bahamian bush – though let me tell you, I'd likely prefer that to all the pomp and circum-stance. But one thing I've learned is that rich people love to be catered to and they love a grand party. I give them one. They buy my flamingos. It's win-win."

"I love a gala!" Miss Elva all but crawled over the table to David and I barely restrained myself from rolling my eyes. "It's a perfect excuse to dress up. What's the theme?"

"We're going with a seventies soul disco this time," David said, tossing his glass of whiskey back like water and signaling to the waiter for another.

"Even better. I have so many sequined things I could wear," Miss Elva laughed, then turned to me. "Her, I'm not sure about."

"I would assume you'd help her," David whispered – which, for him, was the level of a normal speaking voice.

"I do what I can, but you know…" Miss Elva shrugged, as if to say there was only so much she could do.

"I think you look lovely tonight, Althea. The blue is a pretty color," Randall said, smoothly cutting over the awkwardness. Despite his misgivings about my profession, I found him to be perfectly charming.

"Honestly, I'd have to check what we have going on. And find someone to watch Hank. It's a little last-minute."

"Well, you two just let me know. Bring your friends. The more the merrier!" David insisted.

"Would we fly from Miami?"

"Naw, I'd send a plane for you at Key West. Much closer."

"You'd send a plane. For us?"

"Sure. Elva can't be traveling commercial, now, can she? Not a queen like this." David pressed a lavish kiss to Miss Elva's cheek and I swear to goddess she giggled at him.

Giggled.

"We'll let you know," I said, desperate to change the subject and process the fact that I'd just heard Miss Elva simper over a man. Luckily, Beau stepped out from kitchen and made his way to the table. He looked extra handsome tonight, his tanned skin offset nicely by a mint green button-down and white pants.

"Beau, these lovely gentleman just invited us to their gala in the Bahamas next weekend. They say we can bring our friends," Miss Elva all but purred, then she turned to David. "Beau owns this fine establishment and Lucky's Tiki Bar at the end of the strip."

"Both fantastic places," David said, shaking Beau's hand so hard I saw him wince. "You must come for the gala. We'd love to have you."

"That's certainly kind of you to invite me," Beau said, and despite my obvious glare about not wanting to go to the party, added, "I'll have to check my schedule, but I'd love to attend a gala."

"See? It'll be a hoot, won't it, Althea? We'll send the plane," David insisted.

"Yes, they'll send the plane, Althea." Beau turned and beamed at me, ignoring the death stare in my eyes. "I'm sorry, I have to follow up in the kitchen. Enjoy your meal – dessert's on me," Beau said, his attention caught by a waiter motioning to him from the back. Saying his goodbyes, he dipped out, with a wink over his shoulder to me. Traitor, I thought.

Miss Elva giggled at David once more.

"Have you had any updates on your stolen flamingo? It's quite the talk of the town. I'm sorry to hear about it."

Randall's hand tightened on his wine glass, and I wondered it didn't snap in his hand. His lips had thinned, and he pressed them together before inhaling once and forcing himself to calm down. If I didn't know better, I'd say he'd gone from charming to lethal in seconds.

"I'm sorry, I'm still really upset about it. I hate thieves," Randall admitted, taking a large swallow of his wine.

"We both do. But we'll make it right. I've already got another flamingo on its way over to the golf course. It wasn't their fault it got stolen. Sometimes these things happen, though I swear it's been happening more of late. Flamingos seem to be the hot thing right now – which, mind you, I am not complaining about, but with that has come a significant rise in theft."

"More than one flamingo has been stolen?" I had no idea that flamingos were a hot item to take. Who knew there was such an underground world of hidden flamingo thievery? Was there a black market for flamingos? Or would it be a pink market? I did my best not to sputter out a laugh by sucking the rest of my mojito down.

"Yes, lately it's become quite a thing. Namely the larger ones, which as you can imagine is annoying for us. They're more expensive, more difficult to produce, and harder to ship. Randall oversees it all and I know it's been a headache for him, trying to figure out what's been going on."

"That it has," Randall said, and smiled gratefully when the waiter filled his wine up.

"It's a crying shame, that it is. Flamingos are meant to give people joy. Stealing them – well, who has the time? Just ridiculous."

"I have to be honest, I thought it was just kids having a prank," I admitted.

"I would think so too, if it hadn't happened a few times now." David shook his head sadly.

Miss Elva gasped. "Are you saying what I'm thinking?"

"That's right. A serial flamingo thief."

Flocking unreal, I thought, and buried my nose in my drink.

Chapter Eight

"ALTHEA."

I was just diving into the desserts that Beau had sent out – a molten chocolate lava cake with raspberry sorbet for me, perfectly cooked and oozing scrumptious chocolate inside.

Goosebumps ran down my neck. I knew that voice.

"Cash."

Damn it. Why did this man have to look so devilishly handsome every time I saw him? Just once I'd like to see him out of sorts, sweating, maybe with food stuck in his teeth. Anything to make him just a little more like us mere mortals.

"Cash! I haven't seen you in ages. What brings you here?" David slapped a hand on the table, making me jump. Of course he would know Cash. Everyone with money seemed to know Cash.

"I'm having a late dinner with a few of my partners."

I subtly glanced over my shoulder to see a trio of suits at another table. No girlfriend to be seen. I wondered if he was still with his latest girlfriend or if he had moved on. I wondered if he missed me.

Wait. Why was I thinking these things? I *enjoyed* being with Trace. Was it just human nature to want your ex to miss you? Or was I still attracted to Cash? Stubbornly, I stabbed my spoon into my cake, not caring if it was rude to eat while he stood there. It was vitally important for me to eat this lava cake at the correct temperature.

"Are you still considering the investment on Eleuthera?" David asked. I looked up at Cash, interested despite myself.

"I am. I like that it's focused on sustainability and bringing jobs to the locals. A more cohesive and inclusive tourist destination."

"We'll talk more. I'm interested," David said.

"Of course. You have my number. I'm sorry, I just wanted to quickly say hello. I'm being rude to my guests. Althea, you look lovely as always. I hope you're well."

I quickly tried to swallow a mouthful of oozing chocolate and ended up sputtering so hard that Cash thumped me roundly on the back until I could breathe again.

"Yup, well as can be," I sputtered.

Cash smiled his devastating smile at me, and tucked a loose curl behind my ear.

"Good to hear. I hope to see you soon."

With that, he was gone, seeming to take all the air in the room with him. I gulped my water down. Was it hot in here? It felt like it was hot.

"Smooth," Miss Elva muttered, focusing on her key lime pie and shaking her head sadly.

"You know Cash?" Randall guessed.

"Oh, yes. We dated briefly," I admitted.

"Ah. Is this the one you're semi-involved with?"

"No, that's a different one." Great, now I sounded like I got around.

"Hot commodity." David beamed his appreciation at me.

"Just wait until I start putting her in my Elva creations. Then she'll really shine," Miss Elva agreed.

I sighed. "I like my maxi-dresses."

"Of course you do, honey. It's best you stay relatable for your clients and all."

I pinched the bridge of my nose, right where the pressure had begun to build, and wondered how much longer I had to sit at this table.

"So, tell us about being a psychic and all that." David stabbed the air with his spoon, chocolate flying onto the linen tablecloth. "Is it fun?"

"Is it… fun?" I paused and considered that. Usually people asked if I could read their minds or how it worked to see the future. Rarely did people ask me if I enjoyed it. "It is fun. I like helping people find their way, and it's really a beautiful thing to be able to read tarot and see what the future will hold for people."

"That's cool. Can you read people's minds?" Randall asked, his gaze level on mine.

"Nope."

"That's good. I can imagine that would get annoying." Randall smiled at me.

"Right? All those thoughts all day long? Yeesh." I finished my dessert and slid a glance at Miss Elva, who just shook her head at me.

Liar, liar.

Chapter Nine

AFTER A FITFUL NIGHT OF SLEEP, during which both Cash and Trace made appearances in my dreams – proving Rosita correct on the efficiency aspects of more than one man – I woke grubby-eyed and on edge. I was thinking about Miss Elva's warning that a storm was brewing and I couldn't help but feel that the Flamingo King was smack dab at the center of it all.

My phone rang and I rolled over to see Luna's name flash on the screen. It wasn't like her to call this early; usually she would text me, knowing that I wasn't fit for communication before my first cup of coffee. Even Hank rolled over and gave a snort toward the phone before burrowing his nose back under a blanket.

"I've not had coffee," I said into the phone, warning Luna as I pushed my mop of curls out of my face.

"That's fine, I've barely finished mine. I need to talk to you though. I think we have another situation."

"Define situation."

"You know, the situations we seem to have stumbled our way into the past few months."

Luna was being kind. *I* had mainly stumbled my way into situations I shouldn't be involved in and she'd blindly followed, doing her best to keep me from doing something stupid like getting myself killed.

"Talk."

"Miss Elva called me last night and said we're going to the Bahamas this weekend? For a gala? What's the deal?"

"Are we really doing that? I don't even have anything to wear to a gala. As I've been routinely reminded, my fashion sense is lacking."

"It's not lacking, it's just you. And that's absolutely fine, Althea. You know how beautiful I think you are."

"I love you. You're too good for me."

"I know. But keep telling me anyway," Luna's laugh, like angels dancing, made me smile as it always did.

"So are we really going to this shindig?"

"It seems so. Don't worry – I'll help you with an outfit if you need something fancy. However, that's not entirely why I'm calling, though I certainly think it's all connected. And because of that, you and I need to do some magickal prep before this weekend."

"Nooooo," I groaned, punching a pillow with my fist. I'd only recently discovered that I had a few more hidden talents aside from my psychic abilities. A reluctant witch was I, and that was the truth of it. Luna, a white witch who could effortlessly perform acts of great magick with an ease and delicacy that I certainly lacked, was doing her best to train me in her path. Thus far, it had not gone well.

"That's enough, Althea. You'll prepare when I say prepare, and I'll hear no more whining out of you. This is serious." Luna was using her stern voice, which she rarely used. I sat up straighter in bed.

"Something happened."

"Yes, it did. Mathias was working the night shift last night and this morning. He just got home." Mathias, Luna's boyfriend, was a doctor who not only ran his own practice, but also pulled some shifts in the ER at the little hospital downtown. "There were two mysterious deaths this morning."

"Erm… please go on."

"Two bodies were brought to the morgue. Two South American men. They died of mysterious causes. Mathias suspects poisoning, but they'll need to do an autopsy."

"Okay. Why was this mysterious, exactly? Where were they found? How were they found?"

"Chief Thomas found them in a car parked down by the docks. You know how he patrols to make sure there aren't teenagers down there partying or getting into naughty business in their cars. And he found the men in a rental car."

"Just sitting there? Or what?"

"Yup, both sitting in their seats. Windows up. Here's the kicker: There was a deflated flamingo floatie in the back seat."

"Oh." I swear I'm usually more articulate.

"Oh, indeed. No marks, contusions, cuts, anything. Both dead, sitting straight up in their seats, looking at the docks."

"That's not good." Again, not the most articulate, but coffee had still not entered my body.

"It is not."

"Do you think someone is framing the Flamingo King? Like leaving a calling card?"

"I don't know, but I think since Miss Elva is insisting we go to this gala with her, that you and I need to do a little prep work."

"She did give me gris-gris this week," I admitted. Luna gave a sharp inhale over the phone.

"And you're just telling me?"

"I forgot," I admitted, reaching over to scratch Hank's ears. He pulled his nose out from the blanket and glared at me. I understood; I felt the same way when someone tried to drag me from my blankets in the morning.

"I don't like any of this. There's something weird going on with the flamingo people, and now we have murders again."

"How do you know it was murder?"

"Two people don't just die at the same time in their car of natural causes, Althea."

"I mean… it could happen, right? Like a malfunction in the exhaust?"

"Then why the deflated flamingo?"

"Maybe they were going to the beach later?"

"And leave the suitcase of money in their trunk behind?"

"You failed to mention that part."

"You distracted me when you told me Miss Elva gave you gris-gris."

"How do you know all these details?"

"The chief told Mathias. That nasty reporter we don't like was already there, so I'm sure it will be the talk of the town today anyway. I'm just preparing you for it with your clients. Also, clear your schedule by the end of the day if you can."

"I don't wanna do magick." I swear, Sleepy Althea is as petulant as a toddler who doesn't want to pick up her toys.

"Althea Rose, you have been given gifts from the goddess above. It's a shame to her and your lineage to ignore them. A shame, I say." Luna was using her stern voice again.

"Fine. But you're buying me a drink after."

"Better yet, I'll take you shopping for a dress for this weekend."

"Do we have to go?"

"Are you going to let Miss Elva walk into that all on her own?"

"Miss Elva is a strong independent woman who can handle her shit."

"That she is. But even strong independent women need their friends sometimes. And this is one of those times. Now stop whining and go get some coffee."

"Fine, but I'll whine up until I've had the coffee."

"At least I don't have to hear it." At that, Luna hung up.

I peered at Hank. "I don't whine, do I, Hank?"

Hank just grumbled and buried his head further under the blanket.

"I didn't want to say anything, but you have your moments." I swear I almost toppled from the bed before I remembered that Rosita had comfortably ensconced herself in my home. I glared at where she hovered by my bedside.

"Rosita. It's rude to eavesdrop."

"How can I not eavesdrop? Nobody can see me. My very existence means I eavesdrop constantly."

The ghost had a point.

"I can see you."

"And you are well aware I'm staying in your home." Rosita shrugged a shoulder delicately. "What's this about a gala?"

"We're going to the Bahamas this weekend."

"Fun. I hope you'll dress appropriately."

Even the ghost was fashion-shaming me.

"I always dress appropriately."

"That weird hair color says differently."

"What's wrong with my blue streaks?"

"They fade to grey and don't flatter your skin tone. I suggest you go red if you want men to look at you with lust."

Leave it to a ghost to not sugarcoat anything.

"Who says I want men to look at me with lust? I already have a man."

"Do you? Interesting. Well, let's not try to lose him with ugly hair colors, now, shall we?"

I took a deep breath and stared at the ceiling, counting backward from ten.

"Rosita. I need some space."

"Fine. Come on, Hank darling. Let's leave the cranky one to fix those dark circles under her eyes."

Hank bounded from bed, following Rosita with an adoring look on his face.

Traitor.

Chapter Ten

DARK CIRCLES COVERED, coffee consumed, and an appointment booked with my hair stylist, and I was ready for work. Checking the time, I realized that thanks to Luna's early morning call, I had an extra twenty minutes before I needed to leave for work. I hadn't heard from Trace since he'd left for his boat trip, so I decided I'd give him a call before he headed out on his first dive of the day. Wandering to my secret slice of paradise, I settled into the low-slung couch set up on my outdoor patio, where I'd hung twinkle lights and large bamboo fans to dispel some of the humid air. Hank raced down to the beach and back, having found a stick for me to throw.

Finding a beach spot in the Keys was virtually unheard of, which was why I'd bought this place with some inheritance money. I'd taken one look at the semi-detached house and the yard that abutted the water, and had made an offer on the spot. With some serious renovations and a dump truck full of sand, I'd created an actual mini-beach for myself. Hank and I loved nothing more than to spend time outside listening to the water. Take me to the water, I thought, for it always soothes my soul.

Tucking my hair back from my face, I held up my phone to video-chat Trace while also tugging the stick from Hank's mouth and launching it across the yard.

"Hello." Trace's handsome face beamed at me, the blue Caribbean water stretching out behind him, and I smiled automatically in response.

"Hi! How's it going? Did you get settled in?"

"Yeah…" Trace said something and the line broke up a bit, but he was smiling and nodding so I just did the same back.

"You're a little hard to hear. Did you go out on any dives yet?"

"The guests just arrived yesterday. We spent the first day just getting the yacht ready for guests and going over procedures. It looks like it'll be a pretty heavily focused dive charter for some of the guests, which will be fun for me."

"That's cool! I can't wait to hear about it. By the way… I'm going to the Bahamas this weekend."

"For what?" Trace's brows crinkled in confusion.

"Miss Elva's met a man," I said, shrugging a shoulder, "and he's having a gala. She wanted us to come as they've just started seeing each other. We're going with Luna and Beau too, so it'll be a group outing."

"That should be fun. Which island?"

"Eleuthera."

"Good diving there, I hear. Think you'll get any dives in?"

"Not likely if it's a party weekend. I can see, though; maybe there'll be a dive boat going out."

"Well, keep me posted. If you do go out for a dive, and nobody from the group goes with you, just make sure you give them all the details of the dive shop you go with, okay? Better safe than sorry."

"I promise, I will."

"Trace!" A woman's voice giggled behind him and he turned to smile over his shoulder. I raised an eyebrow at the group of young women, clad in string bikinis, that I glimpsed over his shoulder when he turned.

"That's my dive group, 'Thea. I have to get going."

"That's your dive group?" I swear I trust Trace and all that, but those women looked young… and taut.

"Yes, it's a grad school group from the marine biology program in Florida. Daddy dearest is chartering the yacht for daughter and friends."

"They look… nice," I decided.

Trace just smiled patiently at me. "It's fine, Althea. I promise."

"Mmhmm," I murmured, annoyed with myself for being annoyed that my boyfriend – or non-boyfriend or whatever I was calling him – was surrounded by young beauties.

"Hey, I'm not the one refusing to take our relationship to the next level."

"Well, maybe there's a reason for that," I said, nodding toward the group behind him.

"Hey, that's unfair. I'm a one-woman man."

"I know you are, Trace." I sighed and pinched my nose. I'd known Trace a long time. While he'd always been popular with women, he'd never played with more than one at once. "You just didn't mention that your guests would be an all-girl college group."

"I didn't know until last night. They don't tell the workers about the guests until the day of. Yachties are used to just turning over the boat and prepping for the next charter."

"That's fair. I get it. I'm sorry, just having a cranky morning."

"I wish I was there to make you less cranky. I know one thing that cheers you up." Trace sent me a cheeky wink through the phone and I smiled, feeling warmth bloom through me.

"That would be nice this morning. I do have an extra twenty minutes."

"Twenty minutes? Althea, you slay me. You know I can go longer than that," Trace chuckled, then glanced over his shoulder again. "I really have to go."

"Have fun, dive safe!" I called, but he was already signing off.

Hmpf. Rational Althea knew Trace was a good man and he was just doing a job. But irrational Althea was annoyed that it was with plethora of long-legged tanned beauties.

"Let it go, Althea," I said. "He didn't say anything about you going to a big party in the Bahamas this weekend."

"Double standards, indeed," Rosita agreed, making me jump again. "But it's good to keep your man on his toes. He'll wonder about you at this party."

"The only thing I'll be doing at this party is eating expensive food and keeping Miss Elva out of trouble."

"That's what you say now. Island parties have a way of getting people to lose their inhibitions. Trust me, I know."

"My inhibitions are just fine. I'm the least inhibited person you know."

"Trust me, I can tell." Rosita shook her head sadly at my tank dress.

"Seriously? It's a simple black tank dress. There is absolutely nothing wrong with this." I looked down at my dress in confusion.

"Boring."

"Classic."

"If you say so…"

Chapter Eleven

"NOW, we've already talked about creating a circle of protection to practice magick in, remember?" Luna was using her schoolteacher voice this time, and I found it just as annoying as her stern voice. I liked my Luna when she was laughter and light – but she wouldn't be who she was if she didn't also have a steel backbone.

"Yes, Miss." I nodded at her, widening my eyes and pretending to be enthralled with her words.

"Careful, or I'll turn Hank into a rabbit." Luna glared at me.

I gasped. "You would never."

"Of course I wouldn't, I love Hank. But pay attention, please?" Luna asked, pushing up the sleeves of her white silk cardigan. We were located in the back room of her shop, as we'd locked up for the day. In the back room, she had turned her space into not only a storage area for the ingredients she used for making her tonics and products, but a full-on practitioner's studio. With wide-planked wood floors, beautiful lamps, and flowy white linens, it was a veritable magickal playground. I sat on the floor on a slippery teal cushion in the middle of the pentagram marked there, and smiled up at Luna.

"Got it. Protection circle."

"And why do we do that again?"

"So we can channel the flow of your power."

"Right." I still wasn't entirely sure where this so-called flow came from, but apparently I had one.

"What's happened the other times, when you didn't complete your circle correctly?" Luna continued.

"We were cursed –" I bit back my words and glanced at where Rosita glared at me from a corner. "I mean we were blessed with the presence of Rosita and Rafe."

"Right, and while that is certainly delightful, do we need anything else slipping through the veil? For example, perhaps a bad energy?"

"Isn't Rafe already a bad energy?" Rosita laughed in agreement from her corner.

"Just because he annoys you doesn't mean he's a bad energy. He's no demon."

"Ugh, fine. No demons, devils, or anything else of the kind," I promised. Of that much, I was entirely sure. I'd witnessed a few bad energies in my time and I had to say I had absolutely zero interest in toying with any again in the future. Not that I'd chosen to play with any in the past – it had been more like they'd landed on my doorstep like a cockroach, and I'd had to dispose of them.

"After we cast the circle, we'll work on today's lesson."

"Which is?"

"Moving things with your mind."

"Telekinesis."

"Basically. But using magick instead of just mind power. It's telekinesis but with a shot of espresso, so to speak."

"And why this spell, particularly?"

"I asked my pendulum, and this is where it directed me."

"Your pendulum speaks?"

"Althea! I swear you're the worst psychic some-times. A pendulum. You write down your options and see where it swings. I'd asked for guidance on narrowing down the spells and wrote down four. The pendulum selected this one. It's never wrong."

"Out of curiosity, what were the other spells?"

"One for breathing underwater, one for making fire, and one for freezing people in place."

"Honestly, all of those sound useful, and I'm a little offended you haven't taught me them sooner. I might have enjoyed learning magick more. Especially the breathing underwater one. Can you imagine all the money I could save on scuba tanks?" I glared at Luna.

She sighed, crossing her arms over her chest and glaring at me, her delicate features as miffed as I've ever seen them. "You know magick isn't meant to be used for your own personal gain or pleasure."

"Why not? I would be much more inclined to use it then." Luna knew I was kidding, but I couldn't help poking at her.

"Stop distracting me. The sooner we get this done, the sooner we can go dress shopping."

"Why do you think I'm delaying?"

"Oh, stop. You know I can pick an outfit for you in ten minutes flat and have you to happy hour before the sun sets. You are being so dramatic."

"Fine, let's do this."

"Okay, call the circle."

This time I knew I had to take Luna seriously: I didn't think I could stand the presence of another ghost in my life. Rafe was annoying at best, Rosita a some-times-welcome distraction, and I wasn't willing to discover what was behind door number three.

I called the circle as instructed, carefully checking my notes to make sure I got my wording right. I was doing my best to stay completely focused so nothing could break the circle.

"Good." Luna nodded her approval, standing inside the pentagram with me. "Now, this should be a rela-tively simple process as it's something that's first taught to white witches at a young age. If they have an inclina-tion for that particular power, that is."

"What am I moving?"

"I've put a floor pillow on the other side of the room

in the corner. It would be nice if you could bring it into the circle for me to sit on," Luna said.

I looked down to where she'd written the spell in her precise handwriting.

"Okay, focus on the pillow."

"Correct. You want to envision it moving to you in the circle."

"Gotcha. Okay, here goes nothing," I blew out a breath and stared down at the incantation, memorizing it as I brought the image of the pillow to my mind.

"I see the object that I choose,

And I ask the pillow to move.

I direct it as I see,

As I will, so mote it be."

With barely a sound, the pillow torpedoed across the room, slamming into Luna's chest with such force she stumbled back a step. Luckily, she didn't leave the circle and I did my best to choke back a laugh.

"Jesus, Althea, tone it down, will you?" Luna grumbled, tossing the pillow to the floor and proceeding to sit on it in front of me. Reaching out, she grabbed my hands and looked me deep in the eyes. "I've told you that you have more power than you realize. I'm smart, so I chose something soft for you to work on. But if that had been a statue or a plant, you could have really hurt me."

Immediately chagrined, I squeezed her hands.

"I'm sorry. I feel like a klutzy witch who shouldn't really use her powers."

"It's exactly why you *should* use your powers. The more you use them, the more you control them. It's like when you first learned to drive and you kept hitting the accelerator or the brake too hard. In time, you ease up on the pedals as it becomes natural. The same goes for magick. Now, let's run this through a few times until you can gently move objects without them becoming a deadly missile."

"You're right. I'm sorry. If I'm going to learn this, I should do it responsibly."

"That's my girl. You can be impulsive, but you're not stupid. Let's do it again."

"Yes, ma'am."

"Enough with the ma'am stuff. You're older than me."

"Only by three months."

"It still counts."

"Does not."

"Althea! Focus."

"Fine."

Chapter Twelve

"I ONLY KNOCKED the vase off the desk once," I protested, slurping the delicious dredges of my dark & stormy. I'd switched from my usual mojito tonight, as I was feeling kind of dark and stormy after the day I'd had.

"I liked that vase," Luna grumbled, sipping her glass of white wine.

"I'll fix it. Even better, I'll get you a new one."

"I already fixed it, Althea. It's fine."

"I think I did pretty good though," I said, signaling to Beau that I would add one more drink. We were comfortably ensconced at our spots at Lucky's Tiki Bar, waiting for the happy hour rush to die down so we could talk to Beau about the gala this weekend.

As promised, Luna had taken me to a high-end boutique the next town over, after our magickal class where someone, not naming names, had managed to break a vase. The boutique, catering to those who often found themselves off on yacht charters for the weekend, had exactly what we needed for a gala. Well, what I needed. Luna already had several gala-worthy dresses. Apparently, according to everyone who had an opinion this week, I did not.

"The rose gold looks killer on you," Luna said, patting my arm.

"Are you sure? It's a much softer color than I'd usually wear."

"Promise. It's a knockout."

"It's somewhat daring, no?"

"Do you know how hot it's going to be? If there are no island breezes, you'll be grateful for that open back," Luna promised.

Luna had breezed right into the boutique, scanned her way down one rack, plucked out a dress, and ushered me into a fitting room before I could even get through the basic small-town-required small talk with the petite salesgirl. I'd eyed the dress dubiously on the hanger, but knowing Luna was pacing outside, I'd pulled it over my head. Rose gold shimmer fabric that flowed softly over my curves, hugging me in the right places but leaving space and movement in others. It made me feel a little bit like a Grecian goddess, though I would never admit that to anyone. Instead, I'd griped about not being able to wear a bra in the dress – but had purchased it anyway.

"What open back?" Beau pushed a copper mug at

me across the bar, his careful eye having caught that my drink was empty.

"I picked a gala dress for Althea. Rose gold. Shimmer. Deep V-neck. Open back. She looks like a depraved angel."

"Oh, perfect. I can't wait to see it." Beau studied me, tilting his head. "But…"

"What?"

"We're going to get rid of the blue streaks, yes?"

"Yes, fine, I already made an appointment."

"What color are you going?"

"I was thinking red," I mumbled into my glass, not wanting Rosita to overhear that I was taking her advice.

"Hmm, red with rose gold. Maybe you could do rose gold highlights instead? Like a light pink?" Beau asked.

"Would something that light look weird against her dark curls?" Luna asked, leaning back. They both studied me like I was a science experiment.

"Nope, it'll look good."

"I agree. Tell Janice rose gold. She'll know which one." Luna had forced me to go to her fancy salon, insisting that if I was going to keep dying my hair weird colors, I should at least do it the right way, so my hair didn't fall out.

"Fine, fine, fine. Enough about me. I have a dress; I'll do my hair. Luna can do my makeup, it's fine."

"Shoes?" Beau asked, and Luna slapped her hand to her forehead.

"How did I forget shoes?"

"I have shoes," I insisted.

They both ignored me.

"Sparkle or nude?" Luna asked.

"How shimmery is the dress?"

"Like, not sequins. More satiny-shimmery," Luna explained.

"Sequins. Strappy. Not high heels, she'll fall over."

"Wedges. Got it. I know just the pair. I'm in Miami tomorrow so I'll grab them."

"Wait, why are you in Miami tomorrow?"

"I'm going up with Mathias for one of the benefits we do at Children's Hospital."

Luna had taken to going with her boyfriend to the children's hospital, where she worked what subtle magick she could to aid the children in their healing. It took a lot out of her, but I'd never seen her happier. Using her gift for good seemed to light her from within – which was why her products sold so well. They were made not only with magick, but love.

"Fine, I'll take the shoes. Nothing too strappy. I'm clumsy enough without adding any extra impediments to my mobility."

"Oh, we're well aware," Beau promised me, flitting off when someone signaled to him from across the bar.

"Why am I friends with you again?" I called.

"For the free drinks and fashion tips."

"Oh, right," I said, and Luna laughed.

"What's the Flamingo King like?"

"Loud, abrasive – but nice. I think he likes flaunting

his money. He's overly cheerful, but essentially harmless. Kind of like a big dopey puppy dog."

"Interesting. And the son?"

"A charmer. Quieter, watches everything, much more tense. Seemed way more upset about the stolen flamingo than Daddy did. Maybe because he oversees the finances."

"You think he's the brains of the business?"

"Likely, though the King didn't get where he is by being stupid. But I think he largely enjoys the profits of the company while Randall runs it."

"Duly noted. Are we keeping an eye on them?"

"I mean… I wouldn't have thought too much about it. But your news from this morning changed things," I admitted, sipping my rum and mulling it over. "The Flamingo King himself may just be putting on the loud showy act to distract from other dealings."

"Like 'look over here at my ridiculousness so you don't pay too much attention to what I'm doing behind the scenes'?"

"Precisely."

"And Miss Elva has the hots for him?"

"She giggled."

Luna choked on her sip of wine and I smacked her gently on the back.

"She… what?"

"She giggled at the Flamingo King. More than once. I… I don't even know what to make of it."

"Miss Elva is not the giggling type."

"That she is not."

"Oh. Well then. We have some investigating to do. I want Miss Elva to be happy, but not with a shady man who's involved in some dirty business. If she's giggling and not acting herself, perhaps she'd be blind to reading anything on his energy."

"So we go investigate."

"That we do."

"I saw Cash."

"Another detail you left out." Luna could give a strong side-eye when she felt like it.

"Excuse me?" Beau leaned in, and I sighed.

"Do you have ears like a cat?"

"It's my job to hear things in this bar."

"You were there. You knew Cash was in the restaurant."

"Yes, I know that. I'm just trying to figure out why you didn't tell Luna."

"It slipped my mind. We've had a busy day."

Correction: They *both* had strong side-eye game.

"It would be nice if my best friend kept me updated on her life," Luna sniffed, and sipped her wine.

"Ugh. Fine. I saw Cash. He looked amazing, as usual. He told me I looked lovely, I choked on my dessert, he pounded me on the back, and then left me in a puddle of humiliation. Is there anything else you need to know?"

"Yes. Is Trace coming to the Bahamas?" Beau asked, wiping the bar in front of us.

"No, he's on a three-week dive trip with a bunch of beautiful grad students."

More side-eye from Luna on this one.

"What? The man has to work."

"No comment," Luna said.

"I hear my name." Beau disappeared to other side of the bar.

"Again, why am I friends with you two?"

"Because you love us and we love you." Luna squeezed my arm gently and I let out the breath I'd been holding tightly in my chest.

"I do love you both. Goddess help me."

Chapter Thirteen

"I THOUGHT he said this was a private plane," I said, standing on the tarmac of the tiny Key West airport. We'd driven down earlier that day, the four of us in Beau's Jeep, and now we stood in the hot sun, staring at the little eight-seater plane. Where was the red carpet? The champagne? The flight attendants who already knew your name?

"Death trap," Rafe decided.

I whirled on him. "You shut your mouth, Rafe. Just because you're pissy about Miss Elva going to meet a man doesn't mean you have to be a jerk to the rest of us."

"Ohhhh, is someone scared of flying?" Rafe laughed, and I realized my error in letting him see me sweat.

"I'm not afraid of flying," I said, hoisting my tote bag further up on my shoulder as we walked toward the plane. "I just feel like the Flamingo King may have misrepresented the whole 'private plane' thing."

"Ladies – and gentleman." A man, tanned and gorgeous, greeted us by the plane, his smile growing wider as he scanned Beau. "Mr. Lovington sends his apologies. It appears there was a miscommunication and his plane was taken to pick up Ziggy Marley from Miami."

"Uh-huh," I grumbled. I hated name-droppers. But secretly, I was excited. I loved reggae music – and if Bob Marley's son was going to be at this party? Well, it was going to be a damn fine party.

"Well, I sho can understand that. Nobody wants to leave the music at home. That was nice of him to still send us this little plane," Miss Elva said, taking the captain's hand as he swept her considerable girth through the small door of the plane. I'd be lying if I said we didn't all hold our breath a little to see if she squeezed through the door.

"It's a short flight and I promise to get you there safely." The captain poked his head back out the door and held out a hand to Luna.

"That's very nice of you, Captain…" Beau trailed off and smiled up at him.

"Captain Woodley."

"Lovely to meet you," I said, and allowed him to help me up the stairs next. I knew Beau would want to spend a little time flirting with the handsome captain.

Ducking my head, as I couldn't quite stand up

straight in the plane, I took a seat in a row by myself and immediately buckled up, looking around for emergency exits and realizing there was really just the door we'd come through. I'd never flown on a plane this small before, and I suspected I wasn't going to like it.

Here's the thing – I don't hate flying so much as I don't like not being in control. When I'm driving a car, if I screw up, that's on me. But when I'm in a plane, I just kind of have to throw my hands up and ask the goddess to protect us. Growing up, I'd traveled all over the world with my mother's job. She was one of the most famous psychics to the stars, and when they called, she went – for a handsome price, that is. Much of the time, my father and I would go along, neither of my parents having many qualms about pulling me from school, as my dad was a music professor. What I missed in class, he made up for in lessons on the road, and I lived a very fruitful and colorful childhood. Famous people no longer excited me; I'd seen one too many of them in tears at my mother's table, deeply saddened and lonely. Fame had a habit of doing that to people. It made it hard to trust people, and finding love was even trickier. Fame wasn't something I ever sought out, which was why finding myself in the tabloids in the previous months had really bothered me.

Miss Elva, on the other hand? She was built for fame, I thought, as I watched her chatter with Rafe, not the least concerned that the pilot kept glancing at her talking into the air. She never seemed to mind if she was alone for long stretches of time or surrounded by people. She was an island herself, and I imagined she would handle fame quite well – especially when her new fashion line exploded. Which it would, of that I was certain.

"I like him," Beau breathed as he wedged himself into the tiny seat across the tiny aisle from me. Buckling in, he flashed a grin at the captain, who was checking on all his gadgets and doodads in the cockpit.

"I think he likes you too."

"He said he's on island this weekend, I think at the disposal of the Flamingo King." Beau hummed a little, crossing legs clad in faded salmon-pink shorts with tiny palm trees embroidered on them.

"Even better."

"I gave him my number, so we'll see if we can grab a drink later. I guess tonight is kind of like a BBQ or something at a local bar."

"Sounds much more my speed than a gala," I said, wiggling to try and stretch my legs a bit. "Where are we staying again?"

"I called David." Miss Elva turned around and smiled at me. Today she was decked out in a silk caftan covered in a peacock feather design, complete with a green turban with orange crystals embedded in it. "He has us at the house. Apparently, it used to be an old hotel, or like a holiday village. There's the big main house and then a bunch of villas along the water. He put us in our own villa on the estate, so we can join the party easily without having to take a taxi from downtown."

"Old –" I began.

"That's kind of him," Luna said, cutting off my comment.

"Yes, Althea. That's very nice of him. I'm sure the villa will be lovely."

"The place is really nice. You'll have a great stay." Captain Woodley turned and flashed his white smile at us. "Did he say which villa you'd be in?"

"Yes, Villa Tequila, because we're from Tequila Key. Isn't that cute?" Miss Elva cooed, and Captain Woodley's grin widened.

"Good to know. That's a great villa."

"Are all the villas named like that?"

"I think so. He's changed them in the past based on themes. He has a tendency to overhaul the design of stuff when he gets in a mood. This year it's all liquor-themed villas."

"See? That sounds fun. I like him," Miss Elva decided.

"He must like you too. Villa Tequila is the only one with its own infinity pool looking out over the ocean."

"Is that so? Sounds divine," Beau said.

"Oh, it is," Captain Woodley said, and they both smiled.

I looked between the two. Seriously, what was going on with this weekend? Everyone was lovestruck but Luna and me.

"Where's Mathias? On call this weekend?"

"Yes. He needs more notice to get coverage for something like this." Luna shrugged, having adjusted to life as the girlfriend of a doctor.

"That's too bad, I like hanging out with him," I said. I genuinely did. Mathias was one of those rare souls who had a heart of absolute gold and a biting wit that kept me laughing for hours. I don't know that I could have picked a better man for Luna had I tried.

"The pilot likes men," Rosita whispered in my ear, and I jumped.

"Rosita! Stop sneaking up on me."

"I've been here the whole time! How is it sneaking?"

"It just is. You're basically sitting on my shoulder," I grumbled. "It's weird and unnatural."

"So is –"

"I swear, if you say two men being together is weird and unnatural I'll get Luna to ban you back to the other side of the veil," I hissed at her in a low whisper.

"What? No, I was going to say that color on you. I like two men together. I think everyone should love who they want to. Too many people have died for no reason, when love, in any form, is the most natural thing in the world."

"…Oh." I kept forgetting how progressive Rosita was from her years of running her brothel. "What's wrong with this color?" I wore a rust brown dress with light blue stitching at the neckline.

"It makes you look pale. The hair is good. The dress, not so much." Rosita shrugged as if to say there was only so much she could do.

"The hair is good." Luna turned around and looked at my new rose-gold highlights.

"Yes, we were right." Beau perked up from where he'd been typing furiously on his phone. I saw the pilot pick up his phone and grin, and I raised an eyebrow at Beau.

"What? I want to have fun this weekend too."

"Can you not distract the man before he's going to launch us into the air, please?"

"See? I told you Althea was scared of flying," Rafe laughed.

"I'm not!"

"The only thing scarier than flying is that dress you have on," Rafe said. Everyone turned to look at me, except Beau who couldn't hear the ghosts, and was smiling at his phone anyway.

"I honestly don't know what the deal is with the fashion critics this week." I threw up my hands. "Fine. Miss Elva, you can dress me from now on."

"Child, it's about damn time."

Chapter Fourteen

THOUGH I WAS SUSPICIOUS, the trip, as promised, was uneventful and very soon we were touching down on a dusty airline strip with a tiny box of an airport. And by 'box,' I mean literally a one-room airport with ten chairs inside. Nevertheless, we were on land and the flight hadn't been too bumpy. Beau was chatting up Captain Woodley as we walked to a van where a dark-skinned man in a floral shirt held a sign with Miss Elva's name on it. Seeing as we were the only people at the airport, the sign seemed unnecessary, but I appreciated the attention to detail.

"Miss Elva? May I be de first to welcome you. My name is Calvin and I will be your personal driver and concierge dis weekend." Calvin took Miss Elva's hand and kissed it.

"Well, Calvin that sounds absolutely fantastic. Thank you for picking us up and seeing to our needs this weekend. This is Althea, Luna, and Beau. We're all staying in the same villa together, I believe?" Miss Elva chatted with Calvin as he loaded our bags in the van and swept the door open so the cool air inside hit us in a blast.

We clambered in and settled into our seats while Calvin rounded the van. "You hear that? We get our own concierge." Miss Elva smiled back at us, pleased as pie.

"Now, it wouldn't be right if I didn't welcome you to de island without some rum punch, so I'll pour you some now," Calvin said, reaching over to a little blue cooler sitting on the faded front seat. Pulling out a jug, he uncorked it and poured a pinkish-orange liquid into glasses before handing them back one at a time. Bemused, we all looked at each other. We weren't allowed to drink with open containers in the States, but apparently the rules were different here.

"Is it okay to drink this in the car?" Luna asked politely.

Calvin threw back his head and laughed. "Of course it okay. Where else you drink it? In de hot sun? Yes, go on, drink up. I tell you about de island as we go."

We all took a small sip.

"Delicious," Beau decided, and I had to agree. It was the right mix of fruity and sweet, with the alcohol bite just keeping it from being overly sweet.

"How long have you been on the island, Calvin?"

"Me? I move 'ere from Nassau a few years ago. Mind you, I'm a city boy and I prefer de hustle and bustle of de bigger islands. But as I grew older I just kind of slowed down. I didn't want dat no more. When de Flamingo King say, 'Hey Calvin, you come work for me,' I didn't tink nothing of it, you hear me? It was an easy choice. Now I have myself a wife, a nice house, and I'm settled. It's good for my old bones. Don't need to be running no streets anymore. Dat's a young man's game, ya hear?"

"Mmhmm, I hear you," Miss Elva said, and I raised an eyebrow at her. When had she run the streets? Seeing that her glass was already empty, I wondered if the alcohol had already gone to her head.

"Now, Eleuthera? It's a cool island. You stand on de roof of de house and you see both sides. It's thin, you see? Thin and narrow. De main road just runs up and down de island and dat's it. Can't get lost," Calvin said, pointing out various places along the way on the road. He was right – at some points in the road we could easily see ocean on both sides. Along the way he pointed out food stands on the side of the road – those to visit and those to avoid – his favorite bars, and even which tourist shops overcharged. Soon enough, we took a small turn down a dirt road, leaving the pavement behind as we bumped through the low scraggly bush that seemed to hug the island.

"Dis here estate, it's out in de bush. You'll want to watch out for land crabs and snakes. Otherwise, nothing to worry about. But don't go wandering too far into de bush, hey? Dis island, well, it's volcano rock and coral.

Which means there are holes and hidden caves everywhere."

Rafe positively perked up at those words. He opened his mouth to speak, but Miss Elva held up her finger to hush him.

"You're saying we could fall in or you don't want us getting lost?"

"Both."

"Are there any caves we can explore that are like... lighted and stuff?" I asked.

"Sure, there's a few caves on de other side of de island you can go to with ladders in and people picnic in them. They cool, offer shade from de sun. Or you can snorkel to some, if you like dat stuff." Calvin shrugged as he stopped in front of a massive gate where a guard in a booth got out and wandered over to the car. Much like Tequila Key, I thought – nobody moved too quickly if they didn't have to.

"Hey, Calvin. How's Sharon?"

"She good, man. Excited for dis weekend. She likes to look at all de dresses."

"My girl too. Talking this and that about all the famous people. You gone down to Charlie's later?"

"Might do. See what Flamingo King says he needs of us."

"You let me know. I'll pass by if you dere." The guard leaned further into the window and nodded at us, his eyes stopping on Miss Elva. His smile widened and she gave him a cheeky wink.

"Fine woman dere."

"Now you go on. That's de Flamingo King's woman," Calvin said, shooing the guard out.

"He's got good taste."

"Dat he do. Not for you, now, you hear?"

"Sho do. Have a nice day then." The guard waved us through, his eyes never leaving Miss Elva, who sat up straighter and preened.

"He seemed nice," Miss Elva said.

"You watch out for de men here, Miss Elva. They'll be all over a beautiful woman like you."

"Don't I know it, Calvin."

"The one in the back too, with de weird color dress. They gonna like her too."

"It's rust, okay? A rust-colored dress."

"If you say so." Calvin's eyes met mine in the review mirror, then he shook his head sadly as we followed the dirt road further until it once more became paved. As we approached, a row of palm trees sprang up – clearly imported – lining the paved road. The road led to a large fountain in front of a massive pink house, complete with pillars and all. At the top of the steps stood the Flamingo King himself, resplendent in a brilliant pink Bermuda shirt, his rattan hat with its wide pink band, and three dogs of varying sizes at his feet.

"What are those beasts at his feet?" Rafe hissed.

"He has dogs! That's great!" I crowed, hoping they chased Rafe like crazy all weekend.

"It's good to have dogs 'ere. Keeps animals out of

de garden. Unwanted people too," Calvin said with a shrug.

"Where's Hank this weekend?" Miss Elva asked.

"At Miss Susan's." My mother's high school teacher absolutely adored Hank. The feeling was mutual, and I honestly think she was disappointed that I didn't travel more. I had even started considering dropping Hank off there on busier client days so they could keep each other company. I was sure both would be delighted with the arrangement.

"He's not going to want to come back. That woman spoils him," Luna said.

"Hey, I spoil him too."

"You do. Hank has a good life. But he loves you first, and Miss Susan second."

"I was thinking I'd drop him there a few days during the week, since she's all alone."

"That would be nice. You have a good heart, Althea," Miss Elva said as Calvin slid the door open and offered her his hand.

"Elva!" the Flamingo King boomed from the top of the stairs, practically pitching himself down the steps as he raced to greet her.

"Elva?" Luna and Beau whispered in unison, turning to look at me.

I just shrugged. "She allows it."

"Oh my," Beau said.

"I know."

The rest of us piled out of the car while David

fawned over Miss Elva. Turning, he clapped his hands at the sight of us.

"Welcome to Flamingo Estate, where we all flamin-*go* together! Get it?" David threw back his head and laughed, his dogs – all of whom had pink flamingo collars on, mind you – dancing around his feet.

Miss Elva giggled.

Luna and Beau turned to stare at me, and I shrugged.

"I know – I can't flocking believe it."

Chapter Fifteen

"DO YOU SEE THEM?" Luna hissed into my ear as we followed a chattering Flamingo King inside, the dogs loping alongside of us. "They're everywhere."

"What are?"

"Flamingos," Luna said, nodding to the foyer of the house. Calvin had been sent on with our bags, promising to pick us up and take us to our villa once we'd had our tour. I, personally, would have been happy proceeding directly to the villa, but my duty this weekend was to look out for my friend, so I followed David and Miss Elva as he showed her how important he was.

"This is me with Cher. Oh, and here I am with Lenny Kravitz. He has a place on-island, you know. And this is when I was with Bono in Ireland. Nice guy, that Bono. He wanted flamingos for his estate there. Thought it would be a laugh. I got them for him too – sparkly ones! He loved them." David was leading Miss

Elva past a wall of framed photographs and accolades. I quickly learned two things – David always wore pink, and he was quite proud of whom he rubbed elbows with. I wondered if there were any pictures of Randall's mom, and what the story was there.

I peered across the foyer to where Luna had directed my attention and realized she was right. It wasn't as flamboyant as I thought it would be, though, I decided as we moved into the wide main sitting area past the foyer. The floor-to-ceiling windows overlooked the stunningly blue water. Even the sand was pink here, I thought as my eyes followed the long stretch of pink beach below the windows. I wondered if he'd shipped that in, or if it was a naturally occurring thing that happened with beaches here.

The windows were framed by pastel green curtains with what I had originally thought was a pink floral print, but turned out to be an extravagant flamingo pattern. The more I looked, the more they popped out. Light blue sofas with soft pink flamingo embroidery; a brilliant blue rug with swaths of green leaves splashed across it, light pink flamingos peeking from beneath the foliage. In the corner, a gold-plated flamingo table with a glass top held a large glass carafe of water with strawberries and mint floating inside it. Even the standing lamp in the corner was a flamingo with its head tucked into the shade. And somehow it all worked.

"Tasteful flamingo," I decided.

"If that's a thing?" Beau said, leaning in.

"I hope the designer was well compensated for this."

"It would take a genius to throw all this together and make it still work."

"I'm impressed," Luna admitted.

"Flamingo chic, I like to call it," David said, and I jumped, realizing he'd heard us.

"I have to be honest, David. I didn't know flamingo chic was a thing. And if you had asked me to describe it... I never would have been able to. But kudos to your designer. They really nailed it."

"Be sure to tell Captain Woodley that. He designed it."

"He did?" Beau exclaimed and I smiled.

"A man of many talents."

"Indeed he is. Though how he has time to pilot when he does all the designing, I do not know. Says he loves the rush of flying. Gives him a chance to meditate and think of his designs."

"Erm..." Now all I would think about on the way home was my pilot daydreaming about throw pillows instead of having his eyes on the radar.

"Don't you worry, Althea, that man is a professional. He flies me anywhere I ask."

"I'm not worried, I promise. I was just thinking maybe I'd get some design ideas from him," I said, though I didn't think I needed any. I was never one to shy from color, and my house was an explosion of the eclectic that suited me just fine.

"I'm sure he'll love to chat. Nice fellow. Needs a

good man in his life." The Flamingo King shook his head sadly. "I know what it is to be lonely."

Miss Elva put her hand on his arm and David smiled down at her.

"What happened with Randall's mom?" I asked, then paused when everyone glared at me. What? I thought it was the perfect opening to ask about his personal life. Weren't we here to learn more about this man?

"She left me. For the Venezuelan pool boy. Said he had more 'heat' than me. What does that even mean? More heat? Please. I'm a passionate man. About my job, about my family, and certainly about my women." David grinned down at Miss Elva, and I waited for her to put him in his place.

She giggled and squeezed his arm.

I made big eyes at Luna and Beau as though to say, See? See what I'm dealing with here? Luna cleared her throat and followed them as they walked down the sweeping staircase to the sparkling pool shaped like a – you guessed it – flamingo. I could only imagine the pool architects scratching their heads and trying to work out how to configure the design.

"Now, this here pool sure did take us some time. I had to go through several firms, but I finally got it done right. Don't she just sparkle on up?" David crowed, and I had to admit, the pool sure did sparkle in the sunshine.

"I suppose if you have a lot of people, some can

hang out in the leg, if others want to be in the neck. Kind of like a lazy river," Luna said, studying the pool.

"Exactly. Even better on a flamingo floatie," David said.

I met Luna's eyes. I wondered if he knew about the flamingo floatie and the dead men. Granted, it wasn't like he was the only man to know about flamingos – the floaties were all over the place. But it seemed odd to me that they would be in town, have an expensive flamingo stolen, and then two men end up dead with a flamingo floatie.

Flocking funny business up in here, I thought.

"David, I have to ask," Beau said, his aviators shading his eyes and mirroring the flamingo pool, "why flamingos?"

"Well, that's quite the story. Come, let's cool off in the cabana with a tequila and I'll tell you."

"Tequila?" Beau turned to me.

"Sounds flamazing," I chirped, and David laughed, belting me so hard on the back I almost fell over.

"That's the spirit. This one's ready to flamingle!"

Chapter Sixteen

"YOU SEE...FOR a long time, I followed all the rules," David said, one of his staff materializing at his side as we settled on the blush pink cushions in the shade of the palapa by the pool. After ordering a jug of margaritas, he steepled his hands and looked up at the thatched roof. "I lived a staid life. I worked in a private investment firm. I wore tasteful grey suits every day. I had dinner at the country club every Friday night with all the other grey suits. And, if I'm being honest, I was boring myself to death. I couldn't remember a time that I'd truly had fun. Fun for the sake of having fun. For going against the norm. For just being ridiculous."

We sat in rapt attention as two staff members appeared with a tray of glistening margaritas and a bowl of fried conch balls. They placed them on the white wicker table in front of us, then disappeared as silently as they'd arrived.

"Go on, enjoy," David said, waving at the bowl. "Conch fritters. A specialty on-island, though I understand that will likely change soon. Overfished. We need to let the conch population grow again."

I wanted to make a comment about not serving conch fritters, then, but for once I held my tongue.

"So what prompted you to change? There's always a catalyst for a big change like that." I asked.

"I think it was my wife leaving. Well, I'll be honest: She didn't leave, she just had an affair with someone more exotic. More exciting, she said. And I realized she was probably right at the time. But I left her, because trust is really important to me. Randall was in high school, and he wasn't happy with me about it, but he came around. I filed for divorce and then I took a month's leave from my job. I had plenty of vacation time. I ended up on Eleuthera. And instead of doing the drunken party until I can't think straight thing, I just sat on the beach and wrote down what I really wanted out of life. I did my best to think back to the time I had been the happiest."

"And did you find it?" Miss Elva asked.

"I did. It was at my grandmother Doreen's house in Florida when I was little. She was a bit eccentric, but I loved her for it. She had a yard just teeming full of fake plastic flamingos; I used to love running through them as a kid. She would take me to see the flamingos at the zoo and tell me all about them, how they were kind of like pack animals – that you never wanted to see a flamingo alone. That they needed their friends or family or partners around them. And I sat on that beach and realized that was me – I was the lonely flamingo. I hadn't made any friends in the investment world who actually cared about me. My wife hadn't really loved me, just the life that I gave her, and my son was an angry teenager. So what did I have to lose?"

"Your company is the Lonely Flamingo," I breathed, absolutely shocked that I hadn't put it together.

"It is indeed."

"What's that? I'm sorry, I don't know," Luna said, looking between us.

"It's a massive luxury brand that caters to high-end vacations and parties all over the world. Like staging big concerts and picnics or crazy vacations. All focused on community and fun. Family reunions, all that kind of stuff. It's really popular," I said.

"It is."

"So all this didn't just come from selling lawn ornaments," Beau said, and David boomed out a laugh.

"Nope, though I have to tell you that at this point the businesses are about fifty-fifty when it comes to what brings in the most profit. You'd be surprised at the demand for flamingo-themed items. But I tend to let people think all the money comes from that instead of from the party company, because with the party company I meet a lot of famous people and sign a lot of non-disclosures."

"So you built all this so you wouldn't be lonely

anymore." Luna smiled at him, and I knew he'd won her over.

"That's right. Plus, I wanted the fun in life. And what's more ridiculous than bright pink flamingos? Embrace the kitsch, I say!"

"And Randall? When did he come around?"

"It took him a while to work through the angry teenager phase. But I think it was when I was doing a party for P Diddy – or whatever he calls himself now – that Randall suddenly realized I wasn't the awful father who had left his mother in the dust. Unfortunately it took me a few years to get him free of the brainwashing that his mother had done about me. But now we're just fine."

"I'm happy to hear that," I said, though I wondered how much Randall really enjoyed being with his father, versus what his father could offer him.

"I think you've done real nice for yourself, David. In fact, I think I'll make a flamingo caftan just in your honor," Miss Elva said, finishing her drink.

To his credit, David only paled slightly. "I'm sure I'll do my best to wear it proudly," he said, looking a bit worried.

Miss Elva slapped her leg and laughed so loudly we all jumped.

"Not for you to wear, though I sure do appreciate you being kind enough to give it a go. I just mean as a nod to your path and what you've gone through to find your happiness. That's all. Though I could maybe make you a nice tasteful flamingo robe to wear when you get out of the pool?"

"That sounds like a great compromise." They beamed at each other in mutual accord, and I had to wonder if Miss Elva had finally found her match.

"There's Randall now," I said, nodding to where he strode down the steps, looking cool and precise in pressed linen shorts and a collared shirt. Black sunglasses shaded his eyes, and he smiled a welcome as he approached.

"Miss Elva, Althea, Beau – lovely to see you again."

"You as well," I said, and introduced Luna. I could sense his immediate interest in Luna, and I knew she could as well. She would put up a repelling spell soon enough, I thought, and wasn't overly worried that he would bother her this weekend. That's the nice thing about having a witch for a best friend. She might look delicate, but the woman could handle pretty much anything thrown her way.

"It's nice to see you all made it. I hate to interrupt, but there are a few things I need my father for. Would it be okay if we have Calvin take you to your villa? An agenda for the weekend will be in your room, and you can decide which activities you prefer to join. Feel free to ask Calvin to take you anywhere you need; he'll be at your disposal for the weekend." Randall smiled at all of us, but I felt like his smile went a bit flat when he looked at Miss Elva.

Maybe it was the margaritas, or maybe it was the

story that David had just told us. But I had a feeling the Flamingo Kid still had mommy issues when it came to his father and the divorce.

I'd be keeping an eye on Randall this weekend, that was for damn sure.

After a nap in a hammock, of course.

Chapter Seventeen

"THE LONELY FLAMINGO," Rafe scoffed as he zipped about my room later. "No wonder he's lonely. Just look at him."

"Like you're much to look at?" I asked Rafe as I unpacked my suitcase. Rosita laughed from where she sat in the corner, looking dreamily out at the sea.

"I am better than that puffed-up orange man." Rafe straightened his shoulders and threw his head back, while Rosita merely shook her head and chuckled.

"He's not that orange and he's not that puffy. And frankly, even though he's a little over the top, I think he's sweet. I'm glad he shared that story with us tonight," I said as I hung my gala dress in the closet.

Villa Tequila had been as stunning as promised, with an expansive open kitchen and living room, and two wings to the villa – four bedrooms total. I was on the wing with Luna, and Beau and Miss Elva were sharing the other wing. I didn't even care which room they put me in, but was more than pleased with the one I'd been given. The room was done up tastefully in shades of coral pink, white, and sea blue, with only a playful nod to the flamingo theme – a flamingo vase in the corner. I even had my own en-suite bathroom and a beautiful view of the water. There was nothing more a girl could ask for, except maybe a nap, I thought as the two drinks began to hit me. As this was traditionally siesta time in the islands, I wondered if I could sneak a quick nap in or if I needed to show up for anything.

"Did you get your agenda?" Luna asked from the doorway, and I looked over my shoulder to where she stood, holding a white sheet in her hand.

"I didn't. Please don't tell me we have to be some-where right now."

"Nope, now is listed as siesta time. Which, according to this, means nap, pool time, or read in the hammock."

"All of which sound brilliant."

"What will you do?"

"The bed looks nice, but a hammock sounds great as well."

"I'm antsy, not sure if I can sleep. Why don't you nap in the hammock and I'll keep an eye on you from the pool?"

"Why do you think you need to keep an eye on me?"

Luna rolled her eyes. "I'm going to put my suit on."

"Fine, I'll put mine on too." Maybe a dip in the pool would wake me up.

"I've missed this, the blue ocean water here," Rosita said, startling me as I reached to pull my dress over my head and Rafe leered at me.

"Naked women?"

"You're not naked yet. I'm waiting." Rafe crossed his arms over his chest.

I pointed to the door. "Out. Go moon over Miss Elva."

"Don't be cruel, Althea," Rafe said as he huffed off. I looked after him, my mouth agape.

"Pot calling the kettle black," I said, and then rolled my eyes at Rosita's sharp look. "Oh, come on. You know how he is to me."

"That may be, but his heart is hurting over Miss Elva right now. Kindness never goes out of fashion, Althea."

"Remind me when Rafe's been kind to me?"

"I believe he's saved your hide a time or two," Rosita pointed out and I turned away to change into my simple black bikini.

"Tell me why you miss this. The islands."

"I think I've been to this island before. It had a different name then. Rafe will know. We were both here," Rosita said.

I straightened to look at her. "Why were you here?"

"Exploring. There was a big expedition to discover more islands. I needed a break from work, so I came along and helped service the sailors – I'm sure you can guess what that meant. But it was good money and I got to see a beautiful island. There's pirate caves here, as you know."

"How would I know that?"

"Well, the driver man – Calvin? He said there were caves."

"But why do you say they are pirate caves?"

"Because they are. When Rafe remembers, I bet he could take you to them. I wonder if his treasure is still there."

I stopped putting the rest of my clothes away and looked at her.

"You think Rafe has lost treasure on this island?"

"He might. If it's the right island."

"Why is it lost? Why didn't he come back for it?"

"Well, the best-laid plans often go astray, and they *usually* do with Rafe. He plundered from the wrong people. Though he had time to hide his treasure, he was taken away in chains. I'm not certain if that's the ship he died on or not. But nobody knew what happened to his treasure."

"I'm pretty sure it was on another boat. I found it for him. Didn't he tell you that?"

"Any pirate worth his salt has more than one treasure stashed away, Althea."

"Should I ask him about it?"

"I don't know. You just hurt his feelings, so I can't imagine he'd be open to you."

"That's fine; I'm not interested in a treasure hunt right now. I just want to take an actual vacation day and chill at the pool."

"Suit yourself," Rosita said.

I left the room shaking my head. Stopping in the kitchen to fill the reusable water bottle that I took everywhere with me, I saw Rafe hovering in the corner.

"Rafe."

"Beastly woman," he hissed.

"Hey, Rafe. I'm sorry," I said.

He turned to look at me. "Really?"

"Yes, really. I know what it is to hurt over someone. Come join us by the pool. If you're lucky you can look down our bikini tops."

"You promise?" Rafe said, his eyes big.

"I promise. You can hang with us. Don't worry about Miss Elva. You know she'll always love you."

"I suppose I could bring myself to leer at you wenches for a bit," Rafe sniffed, and zoomed past me.

"You're welcome," I called and rolled my eyes all the way to the pool.

Chapter Eighteen

"I COULD GET USED TO THIS," Luna murmured, her head resting on her hands as she leaned against the edge of the infinity pool and looked out over the ocean. Her eyes were shaded by mirrored circle sunglasses that should have made her look like John Lennon, but instead made her petite face look edgy and beautiful.

"It's not like we don't live in our own little paradise," I said, kicking my hammock to swing again, enjoying the light breeze that kept the heat tolerable.

"No, that's true. I think it's just the blue of this water. Or maybe the infinity pool – it adds an extra element of luxe, no?"

"It does. I think having the butler on call really seals the deal for me though." I wasn't going to lie, I'd been shocked when I walked into the main room of the villa to find a man clad in flamingo-pink pants, a white shirt, and matching pink bowtie offering us his services. Beau had about swallowed his tongue, and I had to stop my mind from going down a very naughty road when trying to decide exactly what services he was offering us. To be clear, it was just his margarita-making services. Well, at least that was all he was offering me. The jury was still out for Beau.

"Ladies!" Miss Elva called, and we turned so we could watch her entrance, as she wanted us to. Clad in a sparkling pink bikini – and I do mean sparkling – and an open robe decorated with green-sequin palm leaves, Miss Elva was a walking, talking, disco ball of gorgeousness. When she stepped into the sun, I raised my hand to shade my eyes. I swear, she could have blinded everyone within a mile with her outfit.

"Don't go in the ocean with that swimsuit on," I cautioned Miss Elva as she took off her robe. She draped it delicately on a lounge before wading into the pool.

"You know I don't like salt water, Althea. Bad for my hair." Miss Elva patted her pink turban, covered with – you guessed it – sequins. "But, nevertheless, I'll bite. Why shouldn't I wear this in the ocean?"

"Barracuda like shiny things. They don't see well and they are territorial. I also don't recommend wearing dangly jewelry."

"Hmpf. If some barracuda comes up on me, I'll show him what's what," Miss Elva said, sitting on a low shelf that ran the length of the pool. She tilted her face to the sun.

"I doubt you'd be fast enough."

"You don't know that."

"I like your sunglasses," Luna said, intervening in the conversation. In the shape of pineapples and encrusted in gold crystals, they all but covered Miss Elva's face.

"Thank you. Gucci, you know."

"I didn't, but they are fabulous."

"I wouldn't be wearing them 'round no barracuda, now. They like shiny things," Miss Elva said and sniffed.

"I'll be sure to keep that in mind." Luna nodded her head vigorously. I turned and signaled for our butler/pool boy/waiter guy, and he scurried over.

"A pitcher of margaritas, please, a large carafe of water, and iced coffees as well, if you can manage it, please?" I asked, smiling up at him.

"Of course, Miss Althea. I'm happy to help." With that, he disappeared in a blur of pink and I sighed, wondering if I would actually enjoy having live-in help like this. I suspected I would abuse my power, and become a lazy tyrant of my household, never bothering to clean up after myself or do a load of laundry again. Best to stay humble, I decided.

"What are you nodding to yourself for?" Miss Elva asked, and I snapped back to reality.

"Oh, I was just trying to imagine what it would be like to have 24/7 help at my house. I don't think I'm mature enough for that. I suspect I'd just get really lazy and demanding."

Both Luna and Miss Elva turned to eye me through their sunglasses.

"Excuse me?" I asked, almost toppling out of my hammock as I tried to put my hands on my hips.

"I'm not saying you're lazy," Luna began.

"But you're sure demanding," Miss Elva finished, raising her chin at me.

"People in glass houses…" I murmured.

"Hey, you brought it up, missy. I was just agreeing with you." Miss Elva shrugged.

"I'm well aware of my faults, thankyouverymuch," I grumbled, but perked up when I saw a tray of margaritas working its way toward me.

"I can see the appeal of having help," Luna said, smiling as the butler arranged a table in the shade with our drinks before delivering us each a margarita with crushed ice.

"But you'd never be alone in your own home. I also really like my space," I said, taking a sip of the margarita and enjoying the bite of the lime. Standing, I walked to the pool and sat on the edge, dangling my feet in the water.

"Is that why you don't want to move in with Trace?"

"I guess. I don't know. I'm comfortable in my house. I like what I've built there. I also like that I built it myself, without a man, and created a comfortable space where I can be creative, but also feel safe and cozy when I need to recharge. I love having Trace there when he cooks or spends nights with me, but at the same time I equally love when he leaves and I get my space back."

"That's why you gotta do it my way," Miss Elva said, leaning back to reach for her margarita. "Get your needs met, but never bring them home with you."

"Do you never have a man at your house?"

"Honey, you've seen my house. Now, you know I love it, and I think I decorated exactly as I should to suit my taste. But can you imagine an unsuspecting man walking into that? I mean, I know you all think I'm a bit crazy, but even I know that a man would take one look at all my knick-knacks and hightail it for the door."

You couldn't claim that Miss Elva didn't have a keen sense of awareness, I thought, and yet she continued to surprise me with how clearly she saw herself.

"Plus, no man lives up to me," Rafe boasted from where he'd come to sit by Miss Elva at the pool. "She can trifle with other men, but they aren't in her home like I am."

"That's true, baby. You're my big man, aren't you?"

"That's right, my lovemountain. Why are you even messing with this flamingo man?"

"We discussed this, Rafe, honey. You know I have some physical needs. All women do. Plus, I like him. He needs a friend. You knew those were the rules if I was going to let you stay around," Miss Elva reminded him.

"I know, I know. I just think you deserve better," Rafe grumbled.

I looked around at the gleaming pool and well-appointed guest villa, and opened my mouth to make a comment on just what Rafe could provide Miss Elva that was better than this. But Luna caught my eye and shook her head.

"You just keep on thinking that, lover. You'll keep me on the straight and narrow when it comes to choosing good partners."

"Nothing but the best for you, my lovemountain," Rafe said, his eyes big and adoring.

Ew.

"Rafe," I said, interrupting this gagfest of a conversation, "Rosita mentioned you may have been here before. That you might have a cave here? Where you stashed treasure? Do you remember anything about that?"

"I was thinking this place looked familiar. It's been so long, though…" Rafe said, looking around him. "I can say that this place feels familiar to me, but I'm not sure why. I need help remembering."

"She said you might have been captured here…" I trailed off, unsure if I was bringing up bad memories or not. I wanted to tread carefully so as not to upset Rafe. Despite how much he annoyed the shit out of me, I had to admit he was starting to grow on me a bit.

"Oh!" Rafe zipped into the air and buzzed about like an agitated gnat. When Miss Elva gave me a look, I just shrugged.

"What? I can't protect him from his past. I suspect he would have figured it out eventually. This way maybe we can be there to help him, instead of have it dawn on him at an inopportune moment."

"This is it," Rafe gasped, coming back from wherever he'd disappeared to. I wondered whether he'd managed to traverse the whole island in that span of time.

"Tell me what happened here, baby," Miss Elva said, patting the side of the pool, and Rafe went to sit next to her.

"This was a bad one, I'll admit. I think it is the one that got me killed." Rafe shrugged, seeming at peace with his death now. "I probably deserved it, though. You can only pirate for so long before it catches up with you."

"What did you do?"

"There was an expedition to bring supplies here. The island had already been discovered, but now they really wanted to build on it. It was going to be the next big place to visit, I suppose – Spanish royalty on board. I… I might've stolen from the princess."

"They let the princess come to an undeveloped island?"

"She was a bold woman for her time. She wanted to see the world and stowed away on the ship. She was discovered halfway through, and at that point they were closer to the island than home. I, of course, knew nothing of this when I took her hostage as they came to land."

"Naturally."

"Once I'd cleaned the boat of her treasures, I let her go," Rafe pouted.

"How'd they get you then?"

"I… well, I kind of took a shine to her while I had her in captivity. Now, mind you, I was never one to force myself on a woman. As you know, any woman would come to Rafe's bed willingly."

Rosita snorted from beneath the palapa.

"You don't know anything," Rafe shouted at her.

"I know that my girls loved having you as an appointment because they could just take a nap instead of perform."

"It's because I want a woman to want me," Rafe thundered, darting across the pool at Rosita. "I didn't want to pay for them to come to me."

"Then why were you at my brothel?" Rosita threw up her hands in exasperation.

"Because I was lonely," Rafe shouted.

"It's okay, Rafe." Miss Elva called him back. "We all get lonely sometimes. Those ladies didn't know what they were missing out on."

I couldn't believe our murderous lecherous pirate ghost was really a softie inside. Reserving commentary for later, I sipped my margarita and kept my mouth shut.

"So you liked this princess?"

"I did. She had gumption. You know I like a woman with a strong backbone."

"I do."

"I went back to see her, once they were on land and in camp. I stashed my treasures in a cave I'd found here, which was perfect – there was only one way in or out that I know of. I shouldn't have gone to see her; I knew they would have a scout watching the camp. But something compelled me to. And they surrounded me. I never did tell them where my cave was…"

"Did you get to see the girl?" I couldn't help asking.

"I did. The night before they took me away… she came to see me. Kissed me with her sweet lips and talked to me for hours. It was the nicest night I'd had in a long time. I felt like I mattered, you know? And the next day… well, that was it for me."

"I'm sorry, Rafe," Luna said.

"It's fine, Luna. I remember now that I left this world with a contented heart. For even just a night, I felt like I mattered to someone. For me, that was enough."

"You matter to me, baby," Miss Elva promised.

"So do you, my lovemountain."

Chapter Nineteen

"WOULD SOMEBODY PLEASE COME DRESS ME?" I called down the hallway, having finally thrown in the towel on making my own outfit choices. I just was not in the mood for another slew of comments on my fashion sense this evening.

"Finally!" Beau called as Miss Elva and Luna both emerged from their rooms. They all trudged toward me like they were going to battle.

"Seriously? Is this necessary?"

"Let's just see what we're working with, honey." Miss Elva muscled me aside and scanned my closet where I'd hung my supply of maxi-dresses for the weekend.

"I just would like some input on what to wear for tonight is all," I said, forcing myself not to pout.

"Something that shows your breasts would be nice,"

Rafe commented, then ducked when Rosita lunged at him.

"Althea's not that kind of girl, Rafe. Show some respect."

"I am... I'm respecting her nice boobs. See? That's a compliment." Rafe dodged out of Rosita's way again.

"You don't speak to a lady like that."

"Althea is not a lady," Rafe scoffed. I could see we were back on normal terms.

"He's just jealous that he doesn't get to see boobs anymore," I said.

Rafe snarled at me. "I can see them whenever I want, wench. Remember? Nobody can see me."

"That's creepy. You go and watch people undress without their permission?"

"No, I didn't say that. I'm just saying I could if I wanted to."

"Children, that's enough." Miss Elva pulled a simple blue tank maxi-dress from the closet. "This one is fine, and we'll add some spice. As a basic, it will do."

"Gee, thanks," I grumbled.

"You asked for help, honey. Now just hold on a minute." Miss Elva and Beau disappeared, and Luna turned to smile at me.

"Don't let them get to you, Althea. You can wear whatever you want and own it. It's confidence that makes you beautiful, not what you wear."

"She's right," Rosita mused from her corner. "I had girls who were heavier, not the prettiest to look at, but they carried themselves like they were a delectable sweet that a man would trade his life for. As if they were water after weeks of wandering in the desert. Like they held all the secrets, and the man only had to turn the key. It was never the looks, it was that special something that made a man sit up and take notice. Wear what you want, Althea. Just walk like you have the knowledge to everything. The men, they will follow."

"And let's be honest, Althea. You kind of do have the knowledge. Not only are you beautiful, but you're mysterious – you actually know things. You can glimpse the future. You have actual power. Own that," Luna said.

"But it's not my sole purpose in life to attract a man," I pointed out.

"Even better. It's when you care less that men like you more," Rosita said. "I never needed a man in my life, which is why I had the pick of them when I wanted one. Men sense desperation. They want the one they can't have. Or at the very least, the one who doesn't make it too easy for them."

"I hate to say this, Rosita, because I have the utmost respect for you as a businesswoman. But isn't a brothel an easy place for a man to pick a woman up?"

"For money. But if he could get one of my girls to love him, that was the biggest prize. Giving money was the easy way. Plus, these men knew – the woman who had seen and been with all the men, if she chose him? Well, then he was extra special."

"Here you go." Miss Elva sailed into the room, her arms full of sequins, naturally. "Why aren't you in the dress?"

"Oh, sorry," I said. I pulled my cover-up off and tugged the dress over my bathing suit. Miss Elva just sighed.

"Please put on a nice bra under this."

"I will, but I didn't want to make it too easy for Rafe to see boobs again."

"Ungrateful woman," Rafe said.

"I like this, but maybe this better?" Miss Elva was holding various items against my dress while Luna and Beau leaned together, shaking their heads yes or no. Finally, coming to a conclusion, Miss Elva handed me some pieces.

"Tie this at your waist, your natural waist, then wear this necklace. Leave your hair loose. Neutral sandals."

I looked down at what she'd handed me: a sequined belt in an orange, red, and white hibiscus pattern; and a huge feather statement necklace dripping with silver beads.

"This isn't too much?"

"Just try it."

Pulling the belt around my waist, I cinched it and then secured the necklace around my neck. Turning to the mirror, I was pleasantly surprised by what I saw. I was like a Miss Elva with training wheels.

"I like it. You've kind of taken my dress and made it funky, but still me. I sparkle, but not over the top."

"Right, and it lets your tattoo shine."

I had a beautiful tattoo on the inside of my wrist – Celtic inspired with an evil eye in the center of the design. It was beautiful, and also offered me protection – which, if the last year had been any indication, I needed more of.

"Thank you, my personal consultants. You may go now," I said. "It's time for me to slug this iced coffee and get ready for our island party."

"I kind of feel like tonight will be more fun than tomorrow," Beau said.

"Right? Less pomp and circumstance and more realness."

"Yup. We leave in thirty minutes, everyone. Calvin is picking us up at the door."

"Does anyone need my help with their outfit choices?" I called down the hallway, only to hear three doors slam in response.

"I can't be that bad," I said to Rosita.

"You're not. But it's tough having friends who look like the three of them." Rosita shrugged, her dark curls bouncing.

"Thank you. I have to say, Rosita, it's been nice having you around. Aside from the near heart attacks you give me every time you appear over my shoulder."

"Sorry. I'll try to make a noise or something in the future."

"Thanks. Okay, let's get ready. Maybe I should do a

red lip?" Usually I liked to highlight my eyes, if I wore any makeup at all.

"No. Eyes all the way."

"Yes, ma'am."

An hour later, I was glad I hadn't put lipstick on, because I was tearing into the best BBQ chicken I think I'd ever had. A large crowd of us mingled on the street in front of an open-air bar and grill that had a thatched roof, large bamboo ceiling fans, and a small stage which currently looked like it was being set up for music. Two large grills sat outside the restaurant, where a man with a missing front tooth, a faded Kalik beer shirt, and a cheerful laugh manned the grilling of the meat. Reggae music pulsed from the speakers tucked into the thatched roof, and people had already begun to dance.

Nobody seemed to mind that we stood in the street, and any car that approached was coming to join the party anyway. This was the only building on the street, the only bar I'd seen since we left the estate, and I had this feeling like I'd come to the end of the world. I wasn't surprised when I saw some people dance by me, clearly tourists here for the party, acting as if there were no phones around to record their crazy dance moves. It was just that kind of place – I suppose a little like 'What happens in Eleuthera stays in Eleuthera.'

"They're setting up for karaoke," Beau informed me. Tonight he wore a relaxed linen shirt with a parrot print on it, and faded cargo shorts. He looked at ease, like he could hop behind the grill or mix up a drink at any time, and I supposed that was part of his appeal. Beau just fit in wherever he went, with a cool confidence that I wished I could pull off. We'd been friends since high school, and he'd seen me through my worst moments. I always felt calmer when Beau was around.

"What are you going to sing?"

"Bon Jovi, naturally," Beau said.

"I thought you did Cher." I raised an eyebrow at him.

"Shhh, that's not this crowd," Beau laughed at me.

"Fine, but I'm recording you."

"You will most certainly not."

"I don't see a no phones policy here." I laughed up at him.

"I think the more important question here is – what will Miss Elva and the Flamingo King sing?"

"Ohhh, you think they'll do a duet?"

"Maybe they'll do Sonny and Cher."

"Oh!" I grasped Beau's arm and squeezed it so hard he yelped. "Oh, please, please tell me you think we'll be that lucky! I could die a happy woman if I was treated to that particular spectacle."

"The night is young, my friend, and the rum is flowing. I think we'll be treated to many a spectacle tonight. And if I play my cards right, I may be involved in a scandal or two," Beau said, and I spotted Captain Woodley across the dance floor.

"He's so dreamy," I sighed.

"The best ones are," Beau agreed. "Speaking of…"

I turned as Beau straightened.

"Oh," I said, looking up into a pair of grey eyes that I knew very well.

"Althea, you are looking wonderful this evening," Cash said, his teeth flashing white in his face.

"Erp," I said as I swallowed a piece of orange from my rum punch.

Chapter Twenty

AT LEAST THIS time Beau was the one to pound me on my back while I choked, as if that really lessened my humiliation. Finally, when I could breathe again, I wiped my mouth with a napkin and looked sheepishly at Cash.

And damn if the man didn't just start laughing. Despite myself, I did too.

"I'll just see my way out of this," Beau said. "Cash, tell that handsome brother of yours he can come visit any time."

"He was just asking about you," Cash said.

"Was he now? Isn't that interesting."

"I'm staying out of it," Cash decided.

"Wise man," Beau said and sauntered off, taking my lifeline with him.

"Hi. You look nice," I said to Cash. Of course, he always looked nice. He was one of those men who really *wore* clothes, if you get my meaning. A faded t-shirt or a tuxedo, the man just had it going on. Tonight he looked at ease in a loose button-down with a tropical print, shorts, and sandals. His skin was tanned, his hair a little longer and messier than usual, and a smile that could make a woman think of sinful sweaty nights completed the look.

"Thank you, as do you. But you always look nice," Cash said, his smile slow as he scanned me, heat trailing through my body at his look.

"That's sweet of you, but it has come to my attention recently that I do not, indeed, always look nice." I could hear Rosita scoff over my shoulder and I remembered her words about always being confident.

"Really? How so?"

"It doesn't matter. Actually, I'm feeling pretty great this evening. I love this dress, the food is delicious, and I think I may even dance a little," I said, swaying to the beat of the music, which was increasing in volume as people moved from the eating portion of the night to the dancing portion. Was that Adam Levine who'd just bounced past me? Or perhaps another skinny white guy with tattoos. I craned my neck around and realized that there was more than one recognizable face mingling casually in the crowd of locals.

"Is that right? I always liked it when you loosened up…" Cash's voice was warm at my ear as I scanned the crowd. If I turned, my lips would brush his.

"Did you? I thought that was what you *didn't* like about me," I said, stepping deliberately away.

"There wasn't much I didn't like about you, Althea," Cash said, reaching out to run a hand down my arm. "But I do owe you an apology."

"What for? Specifically, if I may ask?" I looked up at him, and I'd be lying if I said I didn't still have feelings for him. Yes, even though I was happy with Trace. Yes, even though he had hurt my heart when he'd chosen not to be with me. Yes, I'm a confusing person.

"I should have been more accepting of what you do. And who you are. You never hid that from me, and it was what attracted me to you from the beginning."

"Then what changed? Your sister, right? Your family?"

Cash had the decency to look sheepish.

"Listen, they're pretty overbearing. They think they know what's best for me, but it's what they want – not necessarily what's actually right."

"And what is actually right for you?"

"I'm still trying to figure that out." Cash's gaze dipped to my lips and then back up to my eyes. Despite myself, I almost leaned in. Almost...

"Wait, what happened to that beautiful girl you were with at Beau's restaurant opening?"

"Hannah? We realized after a bit of dating that there just wasn't any spark. She's really nice, but not for me. I think she's dating a banker in Miami now."

Figures, I thought. She looked like the perfect banker's wife, all polished and ready to throw a dinner party together at a moment's notice.

"She seemed nice," I offered. See? I can be an adult.

"She is. Just not for me."

I desperately wanted to ask him who he thought was for him. Was it me? I glanced down at my glass to see my rum punch gone, and wondered if the alcohol was loosening my inhibitions too much. It shouldn't matter what Cash thought of me. I was dating Trace. And Trace was… on the other side of the ocean with thirty co-eds.

"Well, thank you for the apology, Cash. I appreciate it." *Put your hands on me.* Eeek! I really needed to tone down my inner slut.

"Is Trace here?"

"No, he's on a dive charter." With beautiful young women, I told myself.

"Are you guys still dating?" Was it just me or was it getting hotter outside? A trickle of sweat dripped down my back.

"Yes, we are."

"Ah." Cash had the decency to back off a bit. "That guy."

"Yes, that guy. He's nice, if you get to know him."

"Not my type," Cash said, earning a laugh from me.

"No, I don't suspect he is."

"Are you guys official?"

"Erm… I don't know." I tilted my head as I thought

about it. Were we? I was the one keeping him at arm's length. But it wasn't like Trace was pushing too hard for anything more. We were comfortable in our holding pattern.

"Does that mean I still have a chance?"

I quickly snapped back to attention.

"Excuse me?"

"I'm asking, Althea," Cash said as he stepped closer. He bent so his lips brushed mine, just a whisper of a kiss. My insides melted. "Do I still have a chance with you?"

"Um…" Coherent thoughts had left my mind.

"I'll take that as a yes," Cash decided. Scooping my glass from my hand, he sauntered away, whistling a merry tune.

I stood there, my mouth gaping open, likely looking like a poleaxed chicken, before Miss Elva rescued me.

"Didn't I say that I should dress you more often?"

"I don't think I can handle it if you dress me more," I said.

"Sure you can, honeychild, just channel your inner Miss Elva."

"And what would my inner Miss Elva say about that?"

We both turned and looked to where Cash was ordering a drink for me, most of the women surrounding the bar openly appraising him.

"I'd say ride that ride until you run out of tickets."

"I'm pretty sure I bought tickets to another ride."

"Child, there's more than one ride at the amusement park."

"I just might not be tall enough to ride this one."

Chapter Twenty-One

"MISS ELVA," Cash said, and handed her a drink. He was good like that, I thought, never missing a trick. Having worked in security before, Cash would have scanned the area, and not much would have missed his careful eye. I wondered if he picked up on anything out of sorts. My gut was telling me I needed to stay more alert this weekend – there was something not right about the Flamingo King and the recent murders. I just didn't know where to start to figure it out.

Honestly, I'd make a crappy detective.

"Thank you, Cash. I certainly appreciate you thinking of me." Miss Elva fluttered her eyelashes at Cash and his smile widened.

"May I say that you are looking smashing this evening?"

"You may, because I know I look fantastic. I saved this one for a special night." Miss Elva twirled so her caftan whirled out and you could see the sparkling print of a tiger creeping through the jungle embellished on her green caftan. A tiger-striped turban – with sequins of course – covered her head, and she'd completed the look with earrings of green and orange crystals that fell in a waterfall to her shoulders.

"You look like you were meant for island living. I see David can't keep his eyes off you," Cash said, rocking back on his heels and taking a long drink from his beer bottle.

"Of course the man can't keep his eyes off me. Not when I'm looking this good. I'm letting him dangle a little bit longer before I go see if he'll karaoke with me. It's a good test of a man's interest, you know."

"Karaoke is?" I asked, raising an eyebrow at her.

"Sure it is. See, you go ask a man to sing with you. It'll show you two things. First, is he willing to go on stage and be seen in public with you – and in a way that might make you look like a couple? Second, is he willing to embarrass himself for you? If so, that's a good sign. You want someone who can laugh at himself, but also go do fun or silly or weird things with you. Karaoke is a great test."

"I had no idea there was such life lessons to be found in karaoke."

"She's not wrong." Cash smiled at me.

"You want to do karaoke with me?" I asked, though the last thing in the world I wanted to do was get up on stage and screech into a microphone.

Cash blew out a breath and ran a hand through his hair, adorably mussing it up and making my fingers itch to fix it. Though I liked him a little messy. He was nearly perfect aside from those personality flaws I had earlier identified in our relationship, and it was nice to see him flustered.

"If that's what you want, Althea, I'd love to do karaoke with you."

"See? He doesn't want to, but he wants you. So he'll get up on stage with you." Miss Elva beamed at him. "Pick a good song, you two; I'll put you on the list."

"Wait!" I called but she'd already disappeared into the crowd, her glittery tiger flowing behind her.

"Well, you've gone and done it now," Cash laughed at me.

"Shit. I hate karaoke."

"Drink up then, because this is gonna hurt." Cash laughed once more and we turned as the music died and someone tapped a microphone.

"Y'all, I have to thank you so much for coming to our little shindig this weekend." Resplendent in a pink linen suitcoat, leaf-green t-shirt, and pink cowboy hat, David addressed the crowd from the small stage. He waited while everyone finished cheering, a pleased smile on his face, and despite myself I found myself cheering too. I hadn't thought I would like him so much, but it was easy to see the obvious joy he found in entertaining others.

"We've got a little treat for you tonight. Not only are

we going to have karaoke" – a cheer went up from the crowd – "but we've got this awesome back-up band for your vocals."

"Is that a famous band?" I leaned in to ask Cash.

"I think it's Ziggy Marley's band, but I'm not totally sure," Cash admitted. Judging by the dreadlocks on the bass player, I thought he might be right.

"I officially regret my decision to ask you to karaoke," I admitted, draining my cup.

"I'll just go refill that," Cash chuckled, grabbing my glass before I could say anything and weaving effortlessly through the crowd. I watched in terror as I saw Adam Levine put his name on the list. Followed by Miss Elva. Followed by – shit, was that Cindi Lauper? There was no way I was howling in my screechy voice in front of a crowd of actual famous singers. I mean… I just couldn't.

Gulping past my suddenly dry throat, I turned to look at the rest of the crowd. My eyes locked on Randall. He stood in the shadows, bending and talking closely with Calvin. They both glanced up at the same time to look at me, and froze when they saw me looking at them. Randall raised a hand in a wave and I nodded in acknowledgement, wondering why I was getting a weird feeling from them.

A part of me felt like Randall didn't like Miss Elva and wanted her away from his father. Which, in turn, led to his slight disgust with me. I could read it, vibrating lightly under the layer of politeness and charm he'd oozed at me at our dinner and ever since we'd arrived on island. I suppose it made sense – Miss Elva and I were about as far away from his country-club-loving mother as one could get.

"Have you decided on a song?"

"We're not really going up there, are we?" I looked at Cash in shock, and he laughed down at me, the low timbre of his voice making my insides go warm.

"We may not have a choice. Miss Elva is a force to be reckoned with."

"Oh goddess," I whispered and slurped at my rum punch. I would need liquid courage for this night.

"Look, there she goes. And the Flamingo King is joining her. I wonder what they'll sing?"

"I hope it's not 'Baby Got Back,'" I said and was rewarded with Cash choking on his drink. This time, I got to pummel him on the back until he could breathe again. Wiping his eyes, he grinned down at me.

"I so appreciate your sense of humor."

"Thanks. I think I'm quite funny as well." I didn't mention that most other people didn't. I'm allowed to entertain myself with my own humor, aren't I?

"I bet it'll be something schmoopy like 'I Got You, Babe,'" Cash decided.

The band began jamming, and Cash and I looked at each other.

"That's the way, uh-huh uh-huh, I like it," Miss Elva belted into the microphone, blowing the whole crowd back with her surprisingly beautiful alto voice. A cheer went up and instantly the crowd began to shimmy, while Miss Elva gyrated across the stage a whirlwind of tiger and sequins. The Flamingo King threw his head back, crowed his approval, and joined her on the vocals. Let's just say... the King should stick to flamingos, I thought. Nevertheless, I got caught up in their act and found myself joining the crowd as we all cheered them on. At some point, another drink materialized in my hand. Cash stayed close, dancing next to me as Miss Elva and the Flamingo King brought the house down.

"I like it!" Miss Elva crowed, and for one terrible moment it looked like she was going to launch herself into the crowd to crowd surf. There was a collective inhale of shock from everyone, and it all released in one loud whoosh when she decided against it and instead launched herself into the Flamingo King's arms. He stumbled back a step, then two, but more power to him – the man held his own. Dipping her low to the floor, he pressed a kiss to her lips while Miss Elva kicked her leg high in the air, showing the entire crowd her satin tiger print thong. As finales went, it was a shocker.

I looked helplessly at Cash and he just shook his head, shrugged, and handed me another drink. There was truly nothing to be said. Luna caught my eye from across the crowd and I didn't even have to pick the thought from her mind to know we were thinking the exact same thing.

This was why we loved Miss Elva.

"Hello Bahamaaaaaaaaas!" A tattooed singer jumped

on the stage, grabbing the microphone and playing the crowd. I was sure I should know who he was, but alas, I wasn't cool enough to put a name to the face. But by the way he swiveled his hips in his leather pants and urged the crowd on, I suspected he'd done this a time or two. Seriously, leather pants in this heat? I hoped he showered before he took a groupie home with him. Ew. The bass player with the dreads kicked off the music for "Play That Funky Music," and the whole crowd went nuts.

Funnily enough, so did I.

It had been a long time since I just let loose, had fun, and didn't think about anything else. I wasn't worried about my clients, about my family, about murders or mysteries or anything else. The only thing that mattered was having fun, right in the now. The music poured around us, the bass thumped, and we all were sweating like we'd been jammed into a sauna together. And not a damn person cared. I began to see the appeal to these hidden island venues – nothing mattered but the music.

At one point, Cash put his arms around my waist and I danced into him, enjoying his touch, not caring about our past or our feelings or anything other than having fun. He had a natural way of moving, confidence in his body and his rhythm that made him fun to dance with. And do other things with, if I remembered correctly – but I wasn't going to be thinking about that, I reminded myself, and finished another drink.

"Althea!" Miss Elva called over the microphone and

everyone turned until they looked at me. "It's your turn."

"Oh no, it's fine, let someone else go," I called and the crowd booed me. Can you believe it? Booed me!

"Nope, your name's on the list," Miss Elva insisted and soon the crowd was chanting my name. I took a deep breath, looked up at the thatched roof of the bar, and then back at Cash.

"You're coming with me."

"Wouldn't miss it for the world, darling." Cash grabbed my hand and dragged me through the crowd until we were at the bottom of the little steps leading to the stage.

"What song are you gonna sing?" Miss Elva crouched down and I whispered in her ear.

"Good choice," Miss Elva said, and turned to speak with the band. They all nodded and before I knew it, Cash and I were staring out at the sea of faces – famous ones at that, mind you – and I felt my throat go dry again.

"Don't look at them," Cash said at my side.

"Some of them do this for a living," I gasped. "And make, like, millions from it."

"So what? That's not your job, they all know that. People just like it when you have confidence and are having fun. Let's have fun, Althea."

Spying Rosita hovering over the crowd, I focused on her and her nod of approval. Who knew I'd get a boost of confidence from a ghost madam? Either way, I felt my inhibitions drop and as the music started, Cash shouted his approval. Turning, we looked in each other's eyes.

"Let's bring this hut down."

"I'm all over it." Shoulder to shoulder, we turned back to the crowd.

"Has anyone heard of a little band called... Queen?"

The crowd went wild.

Chapter Twenty-Two

"I DON'T THINK a single person skipped out on karaoke." I was still giggling on the ride back to the villa, flying on exhilaration and rum, having let loose for the first time in ages. Calvin drove us, chattering the whole way, and the van was much louder on the way home than it had been on the way to the party. We'd acquired a few more passengers, I noted, with Captain Woodley practically in Beau's lap, a few other guests still singing cheerfully in the back, and Randall up front smiling back at us. It had come as a surprise to me that Randall had been willing to karaoke, but he'd gotten up and done a sweetly nervous rendition of Johnny Cash's "I Walk The Line." Despite my misgivings over him, I'd still found myself clapping and cheering for him.

"Nope, and that's the way it should be." Miss Elva adjusted her turban, which at some point in the night had gone askew. "If everyone's in on the joke, it's more fun. That's why I love karaoke. You killed it; by the way."

"Thank you," I said, pleased with myself. I smiled shyly at Cash. He'd made his way into our van, saying that he was staying at the villa next to us anyway. I wondered if he was letting me know where he was on purpose, or what his motives were. Too tired to care, I leaned naturally against him, as the van was at capacity and we'd been squinched all the way down on the seat. "I didn't know about those high notes."

"I don't think anyone even heard us." Cash chuckled and the sound vibrated through him and into my side. "They were all singing just as loudly."

"It's a crowd favorite, that's for sure," Miss Elva said.

"Where's David?" I asked, and saw Randall's shoulders jerk. Yup, I'd read that correctly, I thought, for when everyone had been looking at Miss Elva kissing the Flamingo King, I'd been watching Randall. He'd done a good job of disguising his disgust, but not from me. I could read it all over his energy. Randall definitely had some mommy issues, and as far as he was concerned, Miss Elva wasn't going to be a stepmom anytime soon.

"He stayed to tip the band and pay up with the bar and all that. I think Calvin's going back to get him in a bit." Miss Elva stretched and yawned. "My feet are killing me. I haven't danced that much in ages. I'm going to sleep like the dead tonight."

A little shiver went through me at her words, and I hoped it wasn't a premonition that I should be paying attention to. I needed to talk to Luna when we got back to the villa. It was likely she could do some sort of protective spell around the villa, but I wasn't sure what that would entail.

"Thank you for riding de Calvin Express dis evening," Calvin called as he pulled to a stop in the circle drive, which led to the pathway in front of all of the guest villas. "Please get de rest of de way home safely."

We all clambered from the van, wobbling our way down the path, everyone calling our good nights and goodbyes to each other. I heard one couple whisper about meeting in the pool, and I laughed softly to myself, wondering just how many people would be finding themselves feeling amorous this evening.

"What's so funny?" Cash asked.

I shook my head, realizing that a part of me really wanted to invite him in. We'd stopped in front of our villa, Luna and the others already disappearing inside. Miss Elva had given me one long look before she'd gone inside, carrying her shoes, and I couldn't determine if she was telling me to ride the ride or buy a ticket to a different one.

"Nothing, nothing at all. So, tonight was fun. Thank you for singing with me. It was mildly less embarrassing with you next to me," I said, smiling shyly up at him while all the hormones in my body sat up and paid attention.

"I had fun. Althea... I'd be lying if I said I didn't want to come inside with you," Cash said, stepping forward and running his hands down my arms. Leaning down, he brushed his lips across mine, before angling his head and deepening his kiss. For a moment, I was lost in his taste, remembering how he'd made me feel, my body responding of its own accord. I had a fierce attraction for this man, and that was a fact.

I made myself break the kiss. Taking one giant step back from him, I looked at his lips, which were still wet from mine.

"I... god, Cash. I'm really confused right now. And I don't like making choices out of confusion."

"Trace," Cash said, shaking his head a little.

"Yes, Trace. Even if we aren't fully defined, even if we aren't boyfriend and girlfriend – he's still my best friend. And he trusts me, and I him. As a friend – I can't do this to him. I need the water clear, not muddied, do you get what I'm saying?"

"It does help with visibility," Cash said, and I was reminded that he did dive on occasion.

"Yes, being able to see clearly. It matters."

"Well, may I just say, I'd like to throw my hat in the ring if you're still considering. Otherwise, I hope Trace makes and keeps you happy." Cash bent and kissed my cheek before sauntering away, my hormones screaming in protest as he did.

I swear, at times I hated having a conscience. But I couldn't quite bring myself to take it a step further. Despite what Miss Elva said about life being my playground, I knew that I would hurt Trace if I did go play with Cash. And, as I'd said to Cash, at the base of it all, Trace was my friend. Friends don't hurt each other like that.

Resigned to a lonely night curled up with my morals, I quickly got ready for bed, careful to not leave my room and interrupt any of the party Beau was having down by the pool. Instead, I took a shower to rinse off the sweat and stickiness from dancing all night, pulled on a loose tank and shorts, turned the air conditioning on high, and pulled the cool sheet over my warm body. Despite thinking I'd stay up tossing and turning, the rum did its work and I dropped off like a stone.

I was awakened in the dark by the sound of an airplane directly above our villa.

I sat up in bed and grabbed my phone, checking the time. Three thirty am. What plane was landing at this time of night? Honestly, I hated my curiosity sometimes, but I couldn't just not go outside and see what was going on. Sliding my feet into my flip flops, I padded silently from my room, noting that the rest of the villa was dark and quiet. Everyone must have taken the party to their rooms or passed out. Padding outside, I noticed that all the outside lights were off. Earlier that night, the path that led to all the villas had been illuminated by little white lights tucked among aloe plants and flowers. Now, the path lay in darkness and I made my way via the wan light of the moon.

I gingerly followed the path, catching my toe a time or two and trying not to swear, before I veered off into the bush. Now, you'd think this would have been a good place for me to stop – if I had any sense of survival skills – but no. I continued on, too curious about the plane and what was going on. Maybe I still had some liquid courage pulsing through my system, because I wasn't even thinking about the snakes Calvin had warned me about. Instead, I made my way blindly through the low bush, the plants scraping tracks in my legs, until it seemed I was close to the plane.

The engine sounded like it was directly in front of me, when suddenly it cut out. I only heard a few movements, men whispering, and if I strained my eyes I could just make out the outline of a plane about one hundred feet in front of me. It was a small one, a twin prop, and shadows scurried about.

Finally, my good sense kicked in and I realized that perhaps, maybe, I was putting myself in danger. For there was a reason this plane was landing in the middle of the night, in the bush, with no lights and no announcement. And my dumb ass had wandered right out into the middle of it, because I just couldn't leave well enough alone.

Turning, I began to slowly make my way back to the villa, holding my breath and moving a foot at a time through the bush. Crouching low, I tried to side-scuttle, like a crab.

But I slipped, my foot losing purchase, and I tumbled down a steep embankment into a hole.

Tasting blood in my mouth, I realized that in my effort to keep from crying out, I'd bitten my tongue so hard I'd drawn blood. Tears welled up in my eyes, not because I was all that injured, but in response to my stupidity.

Why did I put myself in situations like this? It was truly none of my damn business what these men were doing with a darkened plane in the middle of the night. Now I was in a hole, my ankle throbbing, and bleeding from my mouth. I wondered how long I'd have to sit here, waiting for the men to leave, before I could limp back to the villa, hoping nobody had seen my exploration into the bush.

Something slithered over my foot and I yelped.

In the next moment, I was blinded by a flashlight being shined in my face. I sighed, holding my hand over my eyes and cursing myself for being too impulsive. Shielding my eyes from the light, I glanced around to see where I'd landed.

Ye shall come here no more.

Written on the wall in thick tacky tar was old school penmanship, and a skull and crossbones. A glimpse of pink in the corner caught my eye, before I was hauled to my feet. Closing my eyes, I faced my future.

"Miss Althea. You can't be out 'ere like dis. I

warned you," Calvin chided me. He ran his hands over me, patting me down.

"I… I'm sorry. I got lost," I lied. "I think I drank too much rum."

"I understand dat. It sho do happen to de best of us. 'Ere, let me help you."

"Erm, okay," I said, honestly not sure if Calvin was friend or foe. What was he doing out here with the plane?

"Did you hurt yourself when you fell? I warned you about caves out 'ere, didn't I?"

"You did, Calvin. I think I wrenched my ankle a bit. I should be okay," I said, stepping gingerly as he helped me back up the embankment. I'd fallen further than I'd realized. I suspected I'd discover a few more bruises in the morning.

"Hold on to me. Slowly," Calvin said, helping me until we were standing on flat land again. He didn't let go of my arm, and I didn't turn around to look at the plane. It was in my best interests to pretend I'd heard and seen nothing.

"Thank you," I said, gingerly moving my ankle around. I'd be limping for a bit, but I didn't think I had done too much damage.

"I'll help you home," Calvin said, hooking his arm around my waist and propelling me forward, away from where I'd seen the plane. "What are you doing out 'ere dis time of night? In your pajamas?"

"Um… well…" I grinned shyly up at Calvin, hoping my act would work. "I was looking for Cash's villa."

"Oh, I see, I see. Dat I can understand. Feeling lonely, were you?"

"I was."

"You need to stay on de path, Miss Althea. De bush, it's dangerous."

"I see that. I got turned around because the lights were out on the path. I couldn't see well and I didn't bring a light," I said, hoping Calvin would believe me and deliver me back to my villa unharmed.

"Dose lights are always tripping a fuse. I tell Mr. Lovington about solar lights, don't I? Over and over, I say – use de solar lights. They cost nothing, and we have plenty of sun. Does he listen? No. Then dis place light up like a palace and de fuse trips."

I wondered if the fuse was helped along whenever a plane landed in the dark.

"Solar definitely seems like a smarter choice. Especially when people have been drinking. I sure did make a poor choice leaving my bed tonight."

"You're okay, Miss Althea. 'Ere we are," Calvin said, helping me up the steps to my villa and stopping at the front door. "You need help to your room?"

"No, thank you, Calvin. I should be okay. Sorry about that – I feel so silly. You did warn me about the caves." I wondered if he could hear my heart thundering in my chest.

"You stay out of de bush. It's a dangerous place."

Calvin's face turned sharp in the light of his flashlight, and I wondered what else he was trying to tell me. For the first time, I felt a shiver of panic race through me.

"Althea? Is that you?" Luna opened the door and I almost cried in relief. I'd been sending her mental images since Calvin had found me, praying she would wake up and read them. It was a little trick she and Miss Elva had taught me, and though I was rusty at it, I did my best to use it when I could.

"Yes, Luna. I took a tumble. My ankle's twisted."

"Oh, you poor thing!" Luna rushed out and put an arm around me, beaming at Calvin so that he automatically smiled at her in return: It was hard not to return one of Luna's smiles – fake or not.

"Calvin saved me."

"You're a right hero, you are, Calvin. Can I get you anything – a drink or some food?"

"No, thank you, ma'am. I'm on my way to bed in a bit and de next guard takes over. Please don't go wandering out in de bush at night. I've warned you." With that, Calvin blinked his flashlight off and faded into the darkness, presumably going about his patrol.

"What the hell happened?" Luna whispered in my ear as she helped me up the steps and to the kitchen, where she shoved me into a chair and put my foot up on another. Flicking all the lights on with a wave of her hand – a power move of hers that I greatly admired – she bent to look at my ankle. "Some swelling. Let me get some ice. Once we treat it the old-fashioned way, I'll see what I can do my way."

"Thank you. Did you get my messages?"

"Yes; we need to work on that. You were basically shrieking in my brain. You woke me from a dead sleep, and I was in total panic until you came traipsing up the steps with Calvin."

"Whoops." I really looked at Luna this time and could see how frazzled she appeared. A thin sheen of sweat coated her perfect face and her hair dared to be out of place. She still looked amazing, just with ruffled feathers.

"It's fine. I'll teach you how to tone it down. I'd rather you alert me you were in trouble than not at all. Again... what the hell?"

"I heard a plane." I sucked in air as she put the ice pack on my ankle, where it simultaneously soothed and burned my skin.

"A plane?"

"I swear to god. It woke me from a dead sleep. I was so confused – what the hell was a plane doing landing in the middle of the night?"

"And of course you felt the need to go poke your nose in somebody else's business." Luna pinched the bridge of her nose, looking pained.

"Well, yeah." I gave her a sheepish smile.

"Althea Rose, where are your street smarts?"

"Hanging out with sober Althea?"

"Keep talking," Luna sighed. She dropped into a

chair across from me. I shifted a bit, feeling an ache in my back that I was sure would be worse in the morning.

"Anywho, I decided to go outside and see what was going on. The lights on the pathway were out, so I just kind of wandered my way closer. It wasn't far from us and I just... I don't know. I wanted to take a look."

"What did you see?"

"There was definitely a plane, a small one, and some men scurrying about in the darkness."

"And how did you fall?"

"I came to my senses at that point and realized I'd likely stepped into a bad situation, so I began to crab-walk out of there."

"Excuse me?" Luna held up a hand to stop me.

"You know... like crouch and side shuffle. Like a crab does."

"Althea," Luna sighed.

"And I shuffled myself into a hole, fell down an embankment, and landed in a cave."

"Of course you did." Luna turned and eyed the bottle of tequila on the counter.

"Yes, go ahead. One for each of us."

"I'm not sure you get any more alcohol if you make decisions like you made tonight."

"Hey, I didn't go home with Cash when he kissed me. Doesn't that count for anything?"

"He kissed you?" Luna stopped, the bottle hovering over two glasses she'd put on the counter.

"Yes."

"And you said no?"

"I did."

"You may have this tequila then." Luna poured us each a generous helping, plopped two ice cubes in, and squeezed a lime over the top. Settling back in her seat, she clinked her glass against mine.

"Talk."

"About Cash or the cave?"

"Both. Cave first."

"So, I land at the bottom of this cave –"

"How did you know it was a cave?"

"I didn't. Not until Calvin flashed his light on me."

"How did he find you?"

"I may have made a little noise when something slithered over my foot in the darkness."

"Ew," Luna decided, sipping her tequila.

"Exactly," I agreed, mirroring her as I let the bite of the tequila burn its way down my throat.

"Was it a big cave?"

"I think it was Rafe's cave," I admitted. "I'll have to talk to him in the morning. But there was old-style writing on the wall, and a skull and crossbones."

"Oh, interesting. I wonder if we could find it again in the morning."

"I think we'll have to be pretty careful. The hole came out of nowhere. And it seems like that area is patrolled."

"Obviously, if they're doing a drug drop," Luna mused.

"Wait, what? Why do you say it's a drug drop?"

"I swear, Althea, do you not watch any crime shows? That's what they do. Planes turn their lights off and land in the bush with someone on the ground using a flashlight. Or they'll drop drums of it out in the water and dudes on jet skis race out and pick it up. It's kind of a thing."

"Honestly, I had never thought too much about the actual logistics of drug smuggling," I admitted. Now I felt even more foolish for having wandered into the bush at night.

"Well, that's what I think it is. Which wouldn't surprise me; there are a lot of rock stars around this weekend. Maybe they needed their fix?"

"Wouldn't most rock stars just bring it with them on their private plane?"

"No clue. I'm pretty oblivious to that world too. I honestly can't believe you didn't think twice about trudging after that plane."

"In retrospect, I'm beginning to see why this was not a smart choice," I agreed.

"You're lucky they didn't kill you. A lot of these guys will shoot on sight, no questions asked."

A shiver went through me at her words. I knew she was right, and it was just now really setting in how stupid I had been.

"I'm blaming the rum. I never drink that much."

"You're lucky. I'm glad Calvin found you."

"Yeah, but why was he out there in the first place?"

"He's security, isn't he?"

"Then why wouldn't he be detaining the plane or whatever?"

"Because it's obviously for somebody who's staying here this weekend."

"Then the question is – who?"

"I think the bigger question I have right now is why didn't you go home with Cash?"

"Ugh," I said, downing the rest of my tequila and letting my head fall back on the chair. "I really, really, really wanted to."

"And… yet?"

"Those were my hormones talking. I can't trust those bitches."

Luna laughed and moved to my foot, removing the ice pack and running her hands gently over my ankle. She muttered a few words under her breath, and I felt a cool balm roll through my ankle.

"There, that should be at least a bit better than what you came in with."

"Thank you, Luna. I love you."

"I love you, too. Now, stay out of the bush and other men's beds."

"I will. Promise."

Chapter Twenty-Three

I WOKE up feeling sore all over, as one would expect from tumbling down an embankment and slamming into a rock wall. My head throbbed, and I wanted nothing more than to roll over and sleep the day away.

"Good morning, sunshine." Beau knocked and then poked his head in the door. Seeing that I had clothes on, he clambered onto the bed next to me and smiled.

"Hi," I said, glaring at him.

"Uh-oh, you need coffee. Back in a jiffy." Beau knew as well as any of my friends not to approach before I'd ingested at least one cup of coffee. Groaning, I pulled myself up so that I was propped against my pillows and gingerly rolled my ankle. Pleased to only feel a small twinge of pain, I silently thanked Luna for her healing powers.

Beau appeared at my door with a gigantic cup of coffee and I smiled my appreciation.

"We leave in thirty minutes. I still have my beauty routine to do. Meet us out front," Beau called over his shoulder. Then he was gone – before I could ask him anything else about what we were doing today. Spying the itinerary on my bedside table, I picked it up and scanned the list.

"Right, island tour," I grumbled, and sipped my coffee, not making one move to get up and get ready. I didn't really need to tour the island and after the night I'd had, I was probably safest just lying in bed and recovering. Decision made, I picked up one of the gossip magazines I'd brought with me and lazily paged through it while I let the coffee make me start to feel human again.

"Uh-uh," Luna said, poking her head in my door.

"Does nobody knock around here?"

"Finish your coffee and get your ass in the shower. I'm not going on this stupid tour alone."

"If neither of us wants to go, why are we going? Let's stay here by the pool."

"While that sounds fabulous, Calvin of 'wanders in the dark bush at night' fame will be driving Miss Elva around today. Are we or are we not going to stick by our friend's side, which is the entire reason we even came on this weekend?"

"Miss Elva's a big girl," I mumbled into my coffee, knowing I was bested.

"Shower. Now."

I showered. Not because Luna told me to, but

because it helped me wake up. I got out and wrapped a towel around me just as my phone rang.

"Trace," I said, smiling as his face filled the screen.

"Hey, pretty lady. I see I caught you at a good time." Trace pretended to leer at me through the phone. "How about a peep show?"

"You wish. You know I don't do that. Knowing me I'd hit the wrong button and go Facebook Live or something."

"You absolutely would. And wouldn't that be a treat for everyone watching?"

"Except for, you know, my parents."

"Yeesh, yeah, you're right. How's the Bahamas?"

"Erm, interesting," I said, flopping onto the bed and giving him a quick rundown. I left out the events of last night so as not to worry him. I felt like it was one of those stories best told in person, so he could see that I was just fine and hadn't banged myself up too much.

"Sounds wild. I'm sorry I'm missing it," Trace said.

"Trace... just so you know, Cash is here."

"That guy." Trace immediately scowled into the phone.

"I know, I know."

"Did you know he was going?"

"I did not. It was a surprise to see him."

"Is he still with that girl?"

"No, he's single now."

"Is he making moves on you?"

"He's... expressed an interest."

Trace's scowl deepened.

"And? Have you expressed an interest back?"

"I've made it clear that we are dating – and beyond anything, we are friends first. I would never do anything to hurt you, Trace."

"I know, I know. He just… ugh, that guy gets under my skin."

"I know he does."

"Listen, if you want to be with him, I don't want to hold you back."

He didn't? This was news to me.

"Um… I didn't say anything about wanting to be with him."

"I'm just saying. If that's what you want. We can take a break and you can see how you feel."

"Wait… what? Where is this coming from? I thought we were in a good place," I said, scrunching up my forehead in confusion.

"We are. It's just… you never want to move forward. And I can't help but think it's me that's holding us back."

"How so? Trace, I'm perfectly happy just how we are."

"But that's the thing… you can't ever keep things just how they are. Relationships have these natural steps. You work toward them together. Being exclusive, moving in together, marriage, kids… all that."

"Is that – are you saying you want marriage and kids?" I was honestly surprised. Trace had never mentioned kids to me in the past. Trace tugged at the knot of hair at the back of his neck, so I knew he was agitated.

"Not, like, *now*. But you know, down the road. I always thought about that. And you're just happy as is."

"But as is – well, it's a good place. We come and go as we please, we cook together, sleep together, dive together. Why can't it be that easy?" I asked, trying to drink my coffee faster so my brain would fire more.

"It can be, but I guess I want more. I don't know. Maybe I don't know what I want," Trace said.

I heard a woman call his name over his shoulder.

"Who is that?"

"Her name is Kelsey. I'm diving with her today."

"Just her?"

"And?"

"I just asked a question."

"You're the one in the Bahamas with Cash," Trace pointed out.

I pulled my head back. "Excuse me, I didn't plan that. He's here on his own accord. And I told you as soon as I talked to you. You didn't mention Kelsey."

"She's a client."

"Is that all?"

"She's expressed an interest."

"Ah, I see." I paused, not sure how to navigate these waters. Waters which were now decidedly low visibility.

"I haven't done anything, Althea. I wouldn't do that

to you." Trace's handsome face looked frustrated and conflicted at the same time.

"I know you wouldn't," I said, automatically knowing it was true. Trace might flirt, but I'd never known him to play around with more than one woman at a time.

"What do you want, Althea?"

"I… I don't know, Trace. I thought we were just fine and enjoying each other's company and going about our lives. I love you, Trace, and would never want to lose you."

"But…"

"No buts. I just don't know what that means from here."

"I don't either. I switch back and forth in my brain between wanting you and putting you in a friend category. We were friends for so long that sometimes I default to thinking of you as that. Then I remember we're more. And then it switches back."

"Do you… do you want to take a break? I mean, I know we aren't like official-official, but… What do you need?"

I'll be honest, it hurt to say that, but sometimes doing the right thing hurts.

"I think what I hear us both saying is we love each other but don't know what moving forward together looks like. Which may mean, moving forward looks like us being friends again."

Ouch. Okay, that hurt more than I thought it would.

"What if we can't go back to being friends?"

"If it's important to us, we will," Trace said. "I don't know what the right answer is, but I'm trying to understand you and what you want, Althea. You don't make it very clear."

"I… I know I don't. I'm conflicted as well. Is it normal to love you but still be attracted to other people?"

"Yes. I love you, but I'm attracted to other people."

"So if that's normal, do we just keep dating and admit we find other people attractive but don't act on it?"

"That, or we become swingers, or we take a break."

"Shit."

Trace laughed. "Althea, I will always love you. You're one of my favorite people ever. But are we trying to force something that isn't right? Or isn't ready? What's going on here?"

"Maybe we are. I don't know. I've never been one to be deeply introspective about relationships." I looked up as Luna popped her head in but, seeing my face, she just nodded and ducked back out.

"I'm giving you a gift," Trace decided.

"What's that?"

"Your freedom. No strings attached. My love is yours. But – you take some time to figure out what you want, and I'll do the same."

"Is this because of Kelsey?"

"Maybe, or maybe it's because every time I hear

Cash's name I can't help but think he'd give you a better life than I could."

"I like my life with you," I protested.

"I know you do. But he could give you more."

"More isn't always better."

"Also true."

"I wish there was a black and white answer here."

"There's not. Emotions aren't black and white. They aren't rational. Everything is shades of grey."

"Where does this leave us?"

"Just on hold, for a little while. Have fun, Althea. Enjoy yourself. I'll do the same. Maybe we're both not quite ready to be fully committed. Maybe we need to get a few things out of our system. If it's meant to be, it's meant to be."

"But what if I say yes and you fall for Kelsey and then I'm desperately missing you and want you back and can't have you?" I asked, clutching at the bedspread, the cotton crinkling under my grip.

"And what if Cash sweeps you off your feet, and pulls out all the stops? I can't compete with him."

"It's not a competition," I said, feeling dangerously close to tears.

"It's not. But I'm being fair to us here, Althea. We both are drawn to other people right now. We're both adult enough to talk it out with each other. I respect that so much, Thea. Most other girls, I'd just break it off. But you and me? Well, I don't know what the future holds for us. We're a lot alike. And I think that's why we can have this conversation. Because neither of us is ready to be settled and we're both dancing around it. I love you, Althea. That will never change – you know that, right?"

"I know, Trace, I really do. I love you too."

"So let's let each other fly a bit. We'll see where we land in a little while, okay?"

"Okay, Trace. You may be right."

"Are you sure?"

"I am."

"Did Miss Elva really sing karaoke?"

"Oh god, Trace, if you could have seen it." I started laughing, despite my feelings of sorrow, and so did Trace.

"Thanks for being you, Trace."

"Thanks for being you, Althea. My best friend, always."

"You too, always."

Chapter Twenty-Four

"WHAT WAS THAT ABOUT?" Luna asked when I entered the kitchen. Miss Elva, Beau, Rosita, and Rafe all surrounded the table, which was filled with fruit and croissants. They all wore equally concerned expressions – well, except for Rafe, who was busy trying to look down the front of the flowy pink kimono-style dress Miss Elva was wearing today. I looked at these people – my people – and loved them so much my heart almost burst.

"Well, it seems that Trace and I are taking a break," I said, grabbing a croissant and ripping a corner off of it. I held up my hands to hold off Luna and Beau who had both made a move to hug me. "No, no hugs. No need for tears. I'm sad, but also I'm okay. It was probably the most adult thing I've done in a while."

"What does 'taking a break' mean exactly?"

"I don't really know. We both acknowledged we

love each other. We said we liked how things were. But neither of us seemed interested in taking things a step forward. Both of us are terrified of losing each other and our friendship. And, well, we both admitted that we're still attracted to other people."

"But that's not abnormal," Luna said.

"Just because you're on a diet doesn't mean you can't look at the menu," Miss Elva agreed.

"I told him Cash was here and has expressed an interest," I said.

"Did he now? I like that man." Miss Elva examined a strawberry before popping it into her mouth.

"And there is a girl named Kelsey on his dive charter who has also expressed an interest."

"Ah, you're both taking a sex holiday. I like it," Beau nodded, as though in perfect understanding.

"It's not a sex holiday. What is that? Do people even do that?"

"Depends on your definition of your relationship. I have friends who are married and have kids. They give themselves one weekend a year – they go to Vegas and either go to a swinger's club or a sex club… something like that. Basically, it's a weekend pass to play with other people. They love it and says it keeps their marriage fresh. Since it works for them, who am I to judge? The only thing I don't stand for is when there's lying going on," Beau said.

"I agree." Luna looked at me and smiled. "Listen, that was a very mature conversation you guys had. And you were honest with him about Cash, he was honest with you about his attraction to this girl. I'd call it a win-win. Unless you're brokenhearted? In that case, I can put a spell on his ding-a-ling."

Beau unconsciously crossed his legs. "Ew, can you do that? And who calls it a ding-a-ling anyway? What are you, twelve?"

"Sorry, it was the first thing that popped in my head. I didn't sleep well. Someone was having midnight wanderings last night." Luna glared at me.

"What did I miss?" Miss Elva looked between us.

"A lot."

"Hello? I'm waiting 'ere for your tour. Is anyone coming?" Calvin called.

"Oh… please, please, please?" Rafe fluttered about the air. "I'd like to see the island again. I think I know where my cave is."

I opened my mouth to tell him that I might know where his cave was, and it wasn't all that far from here, but Calvin stood in the kitchen doorway.

"Is everyone ready? Are we feeling good today?"

His eyes lingered on mine before sweeping down my body to look at my foot. Seemingly pleased with what he saw, he nodded once in my direction. It seemed my secrets were safe with Calvin.

But now I had to wonder just how many secrets he was keeping.

"Calvin, how should we pack for the day? Will we be getting in the water at all?" I asked.

"Best to wear your swimsuit. Dere's a really pretty snorkel spot you can go in if you want. If not, you can sun yourself on de beach. If dat's not to your taste, we can explore other areas. I'm at your disposal."

"I won't go in the water, but you all sure can," Miss Elva said.

"I think someone mentioned caves we can snorkel to?" I asked. Rafe perked up, nodding his head vigorously.

"Sho is – not far from 'ere either. We can do dat and then I take you to de other side of de island? Some nice art stuff dere if you like dat. Helps de locals if you buy a piece or two."

"I prefer to buy from locals," Miss Elva said. "None of that 'Made in China' plastic crap."

"No, no, none of dat at dese shops. I promise," Calvin said, bringing his hand to his heart.

"Then that sounds like a lovely day. Now, Calvin, you know you need to bring me back here in plenty of time to get ready for the gala. I want a small nap, and then begin my preparations. You'd do that for me, wouldn't you dear?"

"Of course, Miss Elva. What de queen wants, she gets."

"I could get used to having you around, Calvin," Miss Elva chuckled.

His smile widened. "It would be a delight," Calvin agreed.

"I'm just going to put my suit on and grab my snorkel gear. I'll be ready to go then," I said.

I needed to get in the water as much as I needed my next breath. Whenever I was upset, I went to the water. While I was content with the decision Trace and I had made, happy even that we'd been able to talk it out in an adult manner, a part of me felt sadness. I wasn't sure why, or what it meant, but nothing like floating about in the water for a bit to help me calm my emotions. Pulling on a simple tank suit, I threw my cover-up over, grabbed a baseball hat, and put my snorkel gear in a tote.

"Show me your secret snorkel spot, Calvin," I called. He smiled as I approached him, but I noticed he scanned me once more.

"You look refreshed today," Calvin said as he held the door for me.

"I iced. No limping," I whispered to him and he nodded his response. I wanted to make it seem like I was keeping everything a secret from the rest of the group. No matter what I'd stumbled onto, it was best that anyone connected with any nefarious behavior thought I was the only one who knew about it. It wouldn't be right to take my friends down with me over my own stupidity.

"Good morning, everyone," Cash said. He was leaning against the van, a loose tank showcasing his tanned muscles, and mirrored glasses shading his eyes. I wanted to climb up his body and lick my way down, and I once again cursed my misbehaving hormones.

"Good morning. Are you joining us on our island tour?"

"I am. The rest of my group went deep-sea fishing, but I'm not really a fan of that."

Score another point for Cash. I couldn't stand sport fishing for any reason. Our oceans were in enough danger from humans without people fishing for trophies. I'd rather a local island man catch a fish to feed his family than some sport fisherman try to catch a prize to stuff on his wall.

"We're going snorkeling first."

"So I hear. I brought my gear."

"We don't have to go far for dis spot," Calvin said, putting the van in gear. Instead of puttering out the main road, Calvin turned the van down and followed a dirt road that paralleled the walking path. Curious, I kept my gaze out the window and tried to see if I could determine where I'd veered from the path the night before. Scraggly green bush stretched across acres of land, all looking the same, and I honestly could not determine where a plane would even be able to land, let alone where I had trudged my way through the bush. Had I hallucinated the whole thing? The scrapes on the inside of my wrist told me differently, though.

There, I thought, looking at a small dirt path where the bush had been pushed aside just a little, at the end of the path past the last villa. That much I did remember – I knew I had walked until I was past the last guest villa. Noting that there was a single small palm tree by the entrance to the path, I tried to make a mental snapshot of the area. There were no other palm trees nearby, and the fact that there was a small one there made me realize it was actually a marker of sorts. I caught Calvin watching me in the rearview mirror and quickly turned my attention to Cash.

"Did you sleep well?"

"I did. It was lonely though." He said the second part softly, and warmth trickled through me. Trace was right, if I was this conflicted in my emotions about another man, I shouldn't be full-on in a relationship. And yet, if I got involved with Cash, what would that mean about my feelings for Trace? Would it be fair to Cash if I had those feelings? I was beginning to think that Miss Elva had it right. Play it light and loose – monogamy was not for everyone.

"That's too bad," I said, looking up at him under my eyelashes. "Maybe you'll be less lonely tonight."

"Is that right? This day just got a lot brighter." Cash's grin flashed in his face and I looked away, trying not to smile. My hormones high-fived me.

Calvin paused the van at the top of a cliff.

"We must walk from 'ere. Is dat all right?"

"I don't mind a walk," Miss Elva said.

"I bring umbrellas for shade, okay, Miss Elva?"

"That's lovely; thank you, Calvin." Miss Elva inclined her head as though she were used to having a butler carrying around her shade umbrella every day of her life. Fake it until you make it, I thought, and swung my gear bag on my shoulder. Together we all stopped at the top of the cliff, gasping at the sight below us. The wind was high here, cutting the heat and whipping my hair around my face. Below us was a perfectly empty and exquisitely beautiful pink-sand beach, tucked into a small cove amongst the cliff walls. The water looked calm there, and I scanned the horizon looking for any signs of a current or undertow. Everything looked calm to me, but I would take a closer look once we were on the shore. Either way, I couldn't wait to get in the water. Spying the path, I darted for it.

"Last one down's a rotten banana!"

"What does that even mean?" Rafe called, flitting after me as I skipped down the path. "Why would anyone be a rotten banana?"

"Because they're last."

"But why? Why call them that?"

"I don't know, Rafe. It's just a saying."

"It's a stupid one."

"Fine, it's a stupid one," I giggled, then gasped as Rosita flitted over my other shoulder.

"Your man is sexy. He looks like he knows what he's doing in the bedroom."

"He does."

"You've been with him? And he's back for more? I'm proud of you. Unlike Rafe here, where the women don't come back twice to him," Rosita laughed.

"Your women didn't. But that's because they couldn't handle all this," Rafe shot back.

"All what?" Rosita said, holding up her pinky finger and laughing.

"You wouldn't know, Rosita; I never asked for you," Rafe fumed.

"I wouldn't have taken you if you had," Rosita shot back.

"That's enough," Miss Elva called down and the ghosts shut up, disappearing to whatever hidden mutual corners they tucked themselves in when they got yelled at. As for me, I was already headfirst into the water, tugging my mask over my face, and letting my favorite place surround me.

Chapter Twenty-Five

"ALTHEA, WAIT," Cash called as I popped back up, balancing on one foot in the water, sliding my fins onto my feet. Since nobody else was going snorkeling, I waited – also to enjoy the view of Cash pulling his tank off and striding into the water, all muscles and tanned skin… and there went my hormones again. On the beach, Miss Elva tipped her sunglasses down and openly checked Cash out, giving me a wink and leering smile behind his back. I could see what she and Rafe had in common.

"Care to join me?" I asked, knowing I likely looked as unsexy as I could be with a mask and snorkel on my head, but not really caring. Cash had already seen every bit of me; I didn't have to put on a show for him.

"I'd love to, thanks for asking," Cash said.

"So it looks like there's a bit of a reef there." I pointed further out in the turquoise water where I could see some lumps of rock and coral under the surface of the clear water. "We'll most likely see some great fish there."

"Where do you think this cave is that Calvin mentioned?"

"Did he mention it?"

"He did to me in the van. But just now on the beach when Luna asked, he said that was at a different beach, not this one."

"And you don't believe him?"

"Nope." Cash grinned down at me, and I stopped to admire the water dripping over the muscular planes of his chest.

"Um, why? Why do you think that is?"

"I like Calvin, a lot. But I think he has his secrets. I'm hoping it's for good reason, but we'll see."

"Why does this interest you?"

"David wants to partner in my investment property here. I take it seriously, whom I partner with. Which means I investigate everyone thoroughly."

"And have you found anything yet?"

"Something's hinky here. I just don't know if it's coming from David or someone else in his organization. In the meantime, I'm just going to keep my ear to the ground and enjoy the party, just like all the other guests."

"Smart guy," I said. "I could likely add a few bits and pieces to your intel."

"Is that so? Care to do so now?"

"Nope. Let's just say that Luna and I came on this trip to keep an eye out for Miss Elva. We're watching as well."

"Grand. We'll reconvene at Lucky's this week and discuss our findings?"

"It's a date," I said, then dipped my face in the water, my cheeks burning. Why did I say the word 'date'? I was in such a weird headspace today.

We kicked out toward the reef, swimming gently in the water, and slowly the ball of angst in my stomach loosened as the water soothed me, as it always did. I loved nothing more than floating in the clear water, watching the fish swim around me, curious as to what I was. The reef here was untouched, and it filled my heart with joy to see it teeming with life, a veritable rainbow of color and activity. Cash and I hovered over the coral, watching as damselfish chased others away from their eggs, parrotfish smiled at us with their big front teeth, and an eel stuck his head out from a hole to see what the fuss was about. It was like spending time inside an aquarium. I felt like I could float for hours, just watching the activity.

Sometimes, when I was feeling particularly creative, I'd make up stories for the fish on the coral, pretending the blenny was a grumpy old man telling people to get off his lawn, or the parrot fish was the geeky kid at school with buck teeth.

Yeah, I can be a nerd. So what?

Cash popped his head up, signaling for me to do so

as well. I had to laugh, he looked so dorky with the mask squishing his face and his hair poking every which way. Which in turn made him even more adorable to me.

"I think I see an opening over here." Cash turned his head and nodded toward a small indentation in the rock wall. "Should we explore?"

"Yes, but go slow – you don't want the waves to slam you against the rocks," I said.

"Yes, mother." Cash grinned and I poked him in the ribs with my finger. Reaching back, he grabbed my hand, and I let him hold it as we kicked over to where he'd seen the opening. His hand felt nice in mine – much larger – and I couldn't help but think that I did like how Cash made me feel protected.

Once we were closer, I could see a clear entrance into the opening. From the shore, it just looked like an outcropping of rocks, but once you swam in front of the rocks you could see the low tunnel cut into the side of the cliff. Without thinking much about it, I swam right into the tunnel, curious to see how far back it went. Cash followed me, as the opening wasn't wide enough for us to go side by side. However, in just a few short strides we found ourselves in a wide-open cavern.

I popped my head up and moved to the side of the cavern, where there were rocks I could stand on. It was hard to see – the only light came from the tunnel we'd swum into, which illuminated the water around us and turned it a brilliant green. Squinting, I tried to see further back into the cave. Without a dive light, though, there wasn't much I could make out. Cash swam up to join me at the side of the cavern, stepping up so he balanced on the same rock as me, the water at our waist.

"Wow, this is beautiful back here, isn't it? I love how the light illuminates the water from below. It kind of reminds me of the blue grotto."

"It's beautiful, but I wonder if there's something more here. I'm dying to know what's further back there." I pointed just as a bat swooped around above, then disappeared into the darkness.

"There's another entrance then, if the bats are coming through," Cash observed.

"Exactly."

"What are you thinking?"

"I think this could be Rafe's pirate treasure cave," I said absentmindedly, and then caught myself when Cash looked at me in question. Sighing, I realized I had to make a decision. Did I just be myself, or hide things from Cash like I had last time?

"Rafe is…?"

"Rafe is Miss Elva's pirate ghost. I can see him and talk to him," I said, and watched his face carefully. Though surprise registered, none of the disbelief or snark that I was expecting followed.

"Okay, pirate ghost. Got it. Can you see all ghosts?"

"No. Currently just two."

Cash looked around.

"Are they here?"

"No, they were hanging with Miss Elva on the beach. But I'll tell you when they're around if you'd like."

"And Miss Elva can see them?"

"And Luna."

"Gotcha. But not Beau."

"No; unfortunately, while I find him to be magickal, he's not *that* kind of magickal."

"Okay, I'm listening, I'm accepting, I'm processing," Cash said, and I smiled up at him. His hands came up around my waist, as if instinctively.

"Thank you for not judging me."

"I'm learning there's a lot more to this world than I can see," Cash admitted. "Though right now, all I can see is how beautiful you look in this light. I'm dying to kiss you, Althea."

"You can kiss me," I said, feeling a bit shy again. Cash paused and dragged his eyes from my lips to my eyes.

"What about Trace?"

"We had a long talk this morning. We're taking a mutually-agreed-upon break."

"You told him I was here?"

"Ah, I did. And that I was attracted to you."

"That's very honest and mature of you."

"I told you he's my friend first. And even if you and I do get involved again, you'll have to understand that I'll always love him. He's been a huge part of my life."

"That's fair, Althea. I wouldn't expect you to throw the people you love out of your life because of me."

"So… yeah. That's where that sits, I guess." Feeling incredibly awkward, I glanced around the cave again.

"Hey, don't be shy. It's me," Cash said, running his hand down my face and turning my chin to him. Before I could think much more about it, he pulled me to him, plastering my wet body against his muscled chest and taking my mouth in a kiss so blistering that I was surprised the water around us didn't start bubbling up. Oh, did this man know how to kiss, I thought, losing myself in the sensation as his hands traced my body, massaging, touching, heat trailing everywhere as he expertly seduced me with his lips. By the time I finally came up for air and pressed myself backwards, my hand on his chest, I was gasping for breath.

"That's a down payment on later," Cash promised.

"I… um…" Great, Althea, way to be smooth, I thought.

"Say yes," Cash said, running his thumb across my lips.

I nipped his finger, watching as his face darkened with desire. "Yes, Cash," I said, smiling up at him.

"We should go before I take you in this cave now."

Eeek! That would be awkward – and everyone on the beach would know what we'd been doing.

"Right, let's go."

"Hey, look." Cash pointed above my head and I turned to see writing on the wall.

"Skull and crossbones," I murmured.

"It looks like it's put up in tar," Cash said, leaning as close as he could to look.

"It's old; I can sense that. I'll ask Rafe. There may be treasure back here."

"Um, should we look around further?"

"How? We have no light. If we try to dive down we'll see nothing, and kick up sediment. And if it's further back in the cave, we'll just hurt ourselves looking for it. Plus, if Calvin is involved in any of this, do you want to come out with armfuls of treasure?"

"All valid points. We'll come tomorrow, with dive lights and whatever other gear I can rustle up. Alone."

"That's a plan. Now, let's go before Calvin gets suspicious."

"What should we say took us too long?"

"Let them think we were being naughty. Better for him to think that than to think we found his private cave."

"Oh, this will be fun," Cash decided and smacked my bum.

I laughed at him and snorkeled out of the cave, feeling all my emotions at once. To say my life was interesting lately was an understatement.

We arrived back at the beach where Calvin stood, a worried expression on his face. As we took our gear off, Cash wrapped an arm around me and gave me a long languid kiss. I blushed and giggled, tucking my head against his chest for a moment, surreptitiously looking at Calvin under my eyelashes. I saw him give us the once-over, smile and nod, and stand down.

Our plan had worked.

"Did you guys just bang?" Beau called.

I shook my head at him. "Beau, what's happened to your manners?"

"I lost them in the bottom of this rum punch," Beau admitted sheepishly, looking down at his glass.

"I mean, you do look like you…" Luna shrugged.

"That's enough, everybody. What happens on the rocks, stays on the rocks."

Calvin looked pleased, relaxation washing through him, and I could only wonder what else he was involved in.

And just how deep I wanted to dig.

Chapter Twenty-Six

THERE WAS no opportunity for me to grill Rafe on his cave, as we were all literally sitting in the same van with the man I suspected was neck deep in a slew of illegal shit. So, instead, I spent the time inching closer to Cash and listening as Calvin regaled us with stories about the locals.

"De shop is here. De one I tell you about. Miss Elva, you'll like Mama Jean. She'll take care of you. I drop you off and be back in two hours, ya? Dere's food next door."

"Fine by us. Thanks, Calvin," Luna said.

We all piled out into the brilliant sunshine, stopping in front of a faded blue building with paint-chipped yellow shutters. A woman, easily double the size of Miss Elva, squeezed out the front door and smiled at us. I heard Rafe's intake of breath.

"Double lovemountain," Rafe breathed.

"Calm down, Rafe," I whispered.

He nodded, biting his tongue for once. I think he was as much in awe of the woman's pendulous breasts and flashy style as we all were.

Miss Elva and Mama Jean stopped and sized each other up. Acknowledging kindred spirits, they nodded in unison.

"I'm Mama Jean."

"Miss Elva." Miss Elva held out her hand, only to be embraced in a big hug from Mama Jean.

"I got de best stuff on island."

"I don't doubt you do. I love your dress," Miss Elva said, following Mama Jean into the shop.

"I made it myself. Come, look at my others." Mama Jean glided back to a rack of floaty dresses bursting with colors.

Miss Elva's eyes bulged. She was in her mecca.

The rest of us filed in, and I had to admit, Mama Jean had taste. Not just in the clothing she offered, but the art on the walls was fantastic. I wasn't sure if she painted it or sourced it from on-island, but there was one particular acrylic print – the sun setting over the water and just the fin of a dolphin peeking up – that captured my heart. It was huge, and I had no idea how I'd get it home, but I wanted it. Circling around, waiting while Miss Elva and Mama Jean debated the pros and cons of a particular pattern, I stopped in front of a case of jewelry. My eyes landed on an intricate necklace, made of quartz stone and gold beads that looked to be an everyday necklace that could be layered or worn with everything. I loved how it sparkled, and I wanted it badly. Not to mention quartz was an excellent conductor for my psychic energies.

"Do you like something?" Cash asked in my ear.

"Oh, I do. This necklace," I pointed. "Quartz is a great stone for channeling your psychic energy. And the dolphin painting, though I have no idea how I'd get it home."

"Let's ask her," Cash said.

"I will, but Miss Elva is having so much fun," I said.

We turned to watch Miss Elva exclaim over a neon pink caftan with parrots scattered across it and little silver discs sewn into the hem.

"That's you," I said to Miss Elva.

Mama Jean beamed. "I was just saying de same."

"I have to tell you, Mama Jean, I think we should work together," Miss Elva said.

Mama Jean leaned backward, crossing her arms over her mountainous breasts, and I thought I saw Rafe's eyes glaze over.

"How so?"

"Well, I'm launching a clothing line. Caftans, high-end resort wear, the works. All bright, all flowy, and everything from high-level fabulous to the more subdued for women who can't quite pull off what we can." They both glanced my way and then back to each other, nodding in unison once again.

"Hey!" I said. "I wear colorful maxis all the time."

"I'm thinking maybe you could consult. Or we could work on designs together, and I'll order the materials and have them made. See, these are nice in a breathable cotton, but some of this stuff I have to make with higher-end materials," Miss Elva said.

"I understand dat, honeychild, I sho do. I can only work with what I get. You get better materials? I make better dresses."

"Do you have an email or are you on the internet?"

"Sure I am, I ship my stuff around de world," Mama Jean said, handing Miss Elva a card.

"What do you say? Are you interested?"

"I say we should have a beer next door and discuss more."

"My kind of woman," Miss Elva said and Rafe almost lost his mind looking between the two of them.

"Before we go over, I'd like to buy a few things," I piped up, pointing to the painting and the necklace. "Though I'm not sure how I'd get the painting home."

"I can ship it anywhere you like. Insurance included."

"We can just take it on the plane. Remember, Captain Woodley is flying us." Beau grinned at me, and I suspected Captain Woodley would happily do anything Beau asked of him.

"Oh, that's right. Great. Is the painter local?"

Mama Jean slapped her knee and bent over, laughing so hard that the chasm between her breasts yawned open and I thought Rafe was going to dive right into it.

"Oh, dat Calvin. He sho is a quiet one, isn't he?"

"Calvin did this?" I was surprised and walked forward to look at the signature in the bottom of corner. Sure enough, I could just make out a 'Calvin' in the scrawled signature.

"He sho did. He's really famous, but he likes to take on other work. Says it keeps him humble."

"I'm shocked. It's beautiful. I'd love to have it."

"And I'd like to buy the lady the necklace," Cash said when Mama Jean began to ring me up. Mama Jean paused, taking in Cash with one long lingering look. Then, turning to me, she nodded her approval.

"That's okay, Cash. You don't have to do that. I can afford it."

"I'd like to."

"When a man wants to buy you gifts, you accept, honey," Mama Jean said, making a *tsk-tsk* noise with her mouth.

"I just don't want men to think they have to buy me gifts," I protested.

"No man thinks he has to buy a woman a gift. He buys a gift if he wants to buy a gift." Mama Jean beamed at Cash. "And dis sexy man wants to buy you a pretty necklace, so when it touches your skin you tink of him."

Oh my, I thought, bringing my hand to my neck. When she put it like that...

"Thank you, Cash, that is very sweet of you," I said.

Cash fastened the necklace around my throat, and I ran my hands over it, loving the cool stones against my neck. Reaching up, I pressed a kiss to his cheek.

"Now, we leave de painting on de wall and take it down when Calvin gets back. Anyone else for purchases before we grab our beers?"

Everyone bought something – Luna a simple tunic in shimmery white that made me think of a pearl straight from the ocean; Beau a jaunty straw hat with parrots on the band; and there were several dresses Miss Elva couldn't decide between so she just took them all. Seeing that Cash was buying nothing, I held a small keychain up when he wasn't looking and Mama Jean smiled, adding it to my total.

Outside we wandered to the open-air bar next door, where the smell of conch fritters and BBQ filled the air. After we'd all ordered a Kalik – even Luna – we settled onto the picnic benches and looked on as Mama Jean and Miss Elva began negotiations.

"I got you something," I said, and slid the keychain across the table to Cash. A grin flashed across his face and he held it up, examining the design. It was a gold-plated shark tooth design and inside it was a small flash-light. It had made me think of him – always on the hunt, and yet incredibly beautiful. I loved sharks, respected their great beauty, and was always impressed with their power. They kind of reminded me of Cash.

"I love it. Thank you," Cash said, flipping the light off and on. He slipped it into his pocket before reaching over the table to play with my fingers. Once Miss Elva and Mama Jean were deep in conversation, I nodded to Luna and Beau.

"We found a cave," I whispered, and motioned for Rafe to stop staring at the women's bosoms and pay attention. He settled in by my shoulder.

"What cave?"

"I found a cave. Last night and today. It has skulls and crossbones in it. In tar on the walls. Sound familiar?" I asked Rafe, speaking quietly over my shoulder. Beau, who was used to me talking to Rafe at this point, paid no mind. Cash, to his credit, looked a little startled but then remembered my words about Rafe.

"That's it, that's my cave," Rafe said into my ear.

"Can you tell me more about it?"

"There's two entrances, I'm remembering more clearly now, though most only know of one – from the land side. But if you swim through a tunnel to the ocean, you can get the loot out. I loved that cave because there were two ways out, and nobody suspected it. It's because there's a sharp turn in the back cavern. But you can get to it."

"Where's your treasure?"

"It's all the way down by the tunnel. If you go in by

the water, you can find it more easily than by land. I hid it that way specifically because nobody would think to go that far into the cave. It was tough, with a torch, because the air was thin back there. The light would keep going out."

"But we can get to it by land? We don't have to snorkel it?"

"You can do both. But finding the land entrance is really hard. I barely remember it."

"I'm pretty sure I fell down that hole last night."

"Even better," Rafe said, nodding his head. "I knew you weren't always a useless wench."

"Gee, thanks, Rafe."

"Um, I hate to intervene here, but what hole did you fall down last night?" Beau asked. I looked up to see both Beau and Cash looking at me with equally annoyed expressions. Luna just shrugged as if to say I was on my own and took a sip of her beer, leaning over to chime in on the clothing conversation the other two women were having.

"Um, yeah, about that."

"You did what?" Cash said, his handsome face darkening.

I quickly filled them in, doing my best to minimize what had happened, but I could see they weren't happy with me.

"Keep it quiet, okay?" I asked, nodding to where Mama Jean expounded on crystals versus sequins.

"Fine, but you can't do that shit, Althea," Beau said, shaking his head.

"I know, I know. I wasn't thinking. I got it." This time I took a long slug of my beer.

"This was the intel you wanted to add to my knowledge?" Cash asked.

"Indeed."

"Well, I'll thank you for it, but could we please be smarter in the future?"

"I blame the rum," I grumbled.

"I blame your impulsiveness," Beau said.

"Why is she impulsive?" Mama Jean asked, suddenly breaking into the conversation.

"I have a tendency to say the wrong things at the wrong time," I said, thinking up an excuse on the fly. "They're worried I'll embarrass myself at the gala tonight."

"I don't tink so. They are plenty of colorful people in attendance tonight. You won't embarrass anyone. 'Specially de Flamingo King. He don't embarrass for nothing."

"Do you like him?" I asked. Might as well get some more intel on him from a local.

"I do like him. He's loud, but I don't mind de loud men. It's de quiet ones I worry over."

"His son's quiet," I observed, and I saw Mama Jean's shoulders tighten up. "Do you worry about him?"

"I said all I'm going to say," Mama Jean said.

Miss Elva glared at me, then turned back to Mama

Jean. "Ignore her. She's just looking out for me because David's taken a shine to me."

"Oh child, you got yourself a live one there." They both slapped the table and laughed.

"Don't I know it, honeychild, don't I know it!"

Chapter Twenty-Seven

IT TURNED out we wouldn't have to say goodbye to Mama Jean for long, as she was also attending the gala that evening.

"Dat Flamingo King, he a nice man. He don't come 'ere and stick his nose up at de locals all fancy-like. He welcomes us all."

"It's de truth," Calvin admitted, smiling as he approached the bar. I hadn't heard him pull up.

"Calvin, Mama Jean tells me you paint. Is she pulling one over on me or are those gorgeous paintings yours?"

"Naw, she not lying. Those are mine. I just like to dabble in my free time. I tink it's good for my brain. I like it."

"Calvin, they're fantastic. I am in love with the dolphin one," I exclaimed.

"You can have it then. No charge."

"Excuse me?" Mama Jean said, putting a hand on her hip. "I'm not refunding this woman."

"No, Calvin, that's not how you do business. I sell my underwater photos too. In fact, all of us are in the business of creating things and selling them, in one way or the other. Your work has value. Please, I insist on paying for it."

"All right, then. Thank you, Miss Althea."

"Can you fit it in the van?"

"I'll go wrap it up now." Calvin disappeared, and we all got up to head to the store. Calvin bubble-wrapped the painting and Mama Jean finished packing up Miss Elva's new clothes.

"We'll see you later." I smiled at Mama Jean, liking her vibe, and we all trooped out to the van.

"Now, I can tour you more, or we go back to the villa so you have a couple hours to get ready for tonight."

"Villa," Miss Elva declared, and I couldn't have agreed more. This girl could use a long luxurious nap in my cool air-conditioned room before I faced tonight.

"But what about looking for my cave?" Rafe hissed in my ear.

"I thought we agreed it was the one by the villa," I whispered back. Cash gave me the side-eye.

"Yeah, but what if I remembered wrong?"

"Then we'll go look for it tomorrow. Honestly, I'm pretty sure this is what you're describing. Just calm down. We'll find it," I whispered, and then held my hand up in his face when he tried to keep chattering at me. Where was Hank when I needed him? My dog would have chased Rafe away for long enough that I could get some peace and quiet.

Luckily, it wasn't a long drive to the villa and soon we were all standing outside in the sun once more, packages in hand, and discussions about the evening going on.

"Hair and makeup will be by at five," Calvin said as he left.

I turned and looked at Luna. "Hair and makeup?"

"The Flamingo King offered." Luna shrugged.

"So that gives us three hours to nap?"

"It does. Especially since you don't have to do your own hair and makeup," Luna pointed out. I could have crowed in delight.

"I'd ask to join you, but I genuinely think right now you'd rather sleep than what I had in mind," Cash said into my ear.

I winced, smiling up at him apologetically. "Don't get me wrong. What you have in mind sounds... exciting." My body flushed at the thought. "But, yes, I'm equally as turned on by the thought of three hours of blissful nap time with nothing to interrupt me."

"I'm competing with sleep these days." Cash shook his head.

"Just today. Not all days." I shrugged. New Althea was working on being as honest as possible. If Cash was going to be interested in me again, he needed to see

Althea unfiltered. Which sometimes meant I'd rather sleep in my ugly pajamas and not put makeup on than have a sexy tumble in bed.

This was one of those times.

"Enjoy your nap. I'm going to have a wander-about," Cash said, which I took to mean he was going to scope for the cave I had told him about. Good; at least I'd have someone else looking for it. I was certainly crap with navigation, and I definitely hadn't been paying much attention to where I was going last night.

"Look for the single palm. I think I saw a path."

"On it."

With that we all traipsed inside. For the most part, we'd mutually agreed we would disappear to our rooms for a rest. Beau looked at me and I knew that face meant we had more to discuss, but for now I just shook my head. I was bone tired and the beer from lunch was making me sleepy. Closing my door, I turned the air conditioner on low and stripped, falling naked into bed and pulling the cool sheet over me. It had been a long night and an emotionally charged day, and all I wanted to do was escape into the sweet bliss of sleep.

"Althea?"

"What?" I shot up in bed, belatedly remembering to grab the sheet to cover my chest, but it was only Luna anyway.

"It's four thirty. I thought you might want a little time to wake up so you don't bite the head off the poor makeup girl." Luna knew me well.

"Oh, phew, okay. Man, I was just lights out there." I blinked and looked around blearily.

"You needed it. Weird day."

"I'd say."

"How are you feeling about it all?"

"I'm... I don't know. I'm worried for Miss Elva. Something's going on here and I don't know who's at the bottom of it. But I also really like the Flamingo King. And I like that Cash is here, and he's already checking into things."

"Is he?"

"Yeah. David was going to invest with him in his new resort, but Cash is careful about who he partners with. He's here poking around."

"That makes me feel better."

"Me too."

"Does he make you feel safe?"

"He does."

"What are you going to do about him?"

"I don't know. I'm beyond attracted to him. It isn't attraction that's the issue. It's me fitting into his world. This time around, if we do date for a bit, I'm going to be as open and unfiltered Althea as I can be."

"That's the way you should always be."

"But I still have feelings for Trace."

"Of course you do."

"I'm confused. I feel like I'm doing something wrong."

"Have you lied to either man?"

"Nope."

"Have you been honest about your feelings for both?"

"Mostly. My feelings for Cash are murky, but he knows I'm attracted to him."

"As long as you walk your path in truth, then you're doing nothing wrong. Just don't play games, be honest, and do what feels right for you in the moment. That's all any of us can do, Althea. There's no right answer in how you navigate relationships. So long as you're honest."

"I'm not a good liar."

"Nope. You're complete shit at lying."

"So you're saying that so long as I'm truthful with everyone, I can sleep with Cash?"

"As long as everyone knows the score. If Cash still wants to step up to bat, then I'd say have fun."

"Huh. Well, then. Tonight just got a lot more interesting."

"That it did. And you're going to look stunning. Cash is going to swallow his tongue when he sees you."

"I can't wait."

"Me either. Now get in the shower and have a cup of coffee so your brain is working."

"Luna?"

"Yes?" Luna stopped and looked back in at me. My heart swelled with loving her so much.

"I love you. In case I don't tell you enough. You're the best friend I could have. I'm blessed to have you in my life."

"Althea, that's really sweet of you," Luna said, coming back in and giving me a big hug. "I love you too."

"I told you I'm being open and honest. I just realized that maybe I didn't say that enough to my friends. I don't want you to think I take you for granted."

"I know you don't. I'm honored to call you my friend too."

"Really?" I asked, and tears spiked my eyes.

"Don't you dare," Luna warned, glaring at the sheen that filled my eyes.

"I'm doing nothing. It's nothing," I promised, getting up and streaking toward the bathroom. "Damn air conditioner messing with my allergies."

"Nice butt," Luna called into the bathroom, and I laughed so hard that I did cry this time.

That's what friends were for, after all.

Chapter Twenty-Eight

"I DON'T GET what the point of all this is," I complained to Luna. "I'm just going to sweat it all off."

"No you won't," the makeup girl, Irene, promised. "I do all the beach weddings here. You just put a little milk of magnesia on the skin first and then we do a spray foundation."

"I'm not getting married though. So why the fuss?"

"Because every once in a while it's nice to dress up and make yourself look beautiful. Not that you're not beautiful every day, but it's nice to showcase the goods once in a while," Irene said. Then I had to shut my mouth because she was spraying stuff on my face.

"It's fun to be a little extra once in a while," Luna said from across the kitchen table where she was getting her hair curled. "Plus, you have a sexy man who can see you all dolled up, so that's an added bonus."

"Sexy men are always an added bonus," Irene agreed.

"Hers is hot. He looks like Channing Tatum," Luna said.

Irene paused. "I saw him earlier! He was wandering around outside in that hot sun. I think when he took his shirt off the entire van of makeup girls cheered."

"That would be the one," I said and smiled.

"Damn, girl," Irene said. Succinct, she was.

"Indeed."

"What are you wearing tonight?" the hair girl, Lisa, asked me.

"A rose gold gown. Shimmery."

"Perfect. We'll just work with your curls, because this humidity is a nightmare. I'll just touch them up a bit, and we'll maybe braid it back on one side, sweeping it over the other shoulder?"

"You're the boss," I said with a shrug.

"It'll be great, trust me," Lisa said. Her hair was done up in a series of intricate braids, with beads woven through. It looked complicated and exotic, so I did indeed trust her.

"Done," Irene said, and she and Lisa switched. Lisa chattered away about the party as she deftly braided and curled my hair. In what felt like no time, I was pronounced ready to go.

"I'll help you with your dress, and you with mine," Luna said. Lisa had swept her blond hair back into a low loose bun, one of those ones that looked effortless, but took forever to make perfect. A few wisps of hair were artfully left out, and her makeup made her blue eyes huge in her face.

"You look like an angel."

"Just wait until you see my dress."

I followed Luna into her room and laughed at the sexy fringy short white beaded dress she had hanging on the closet door.

"Is this gala-appropriate?"

"It's a seventies soul gala," Luna reminded me and I held the dress over her head and zipped her up. Turning, she struck a pose, and I smiled as all the fringes on her dress sparkled and moved.

"It's perfect. You now look like a disco witch."

"Even better. I'm ready to bust out some soul moves tonight."

"I can't wait."

"Here, let me get you in your dress. Then I want to have a quick video chat with Mathias so he can see how good I look and make him miss me even more."

"That man is besotted with you already."

"I know. But since he can't be here, I like to include him all I can. Plus it makes my welcome home that much sweeter… and naughtier."

"Thatta girl," I said and held my arms up while Luna helped me into the shimmery rose gold gown, securing the shoulder and the side zip so that it draped over me in one fluid column. Standing back, Luna whistled.

"Cash is going to swallow his tongue."

"I hope not, I have plans for that tongue."

"Althea Rose!" Beau chided from the doorway, and I turned, blushing but also laughing.

"Sorry, that was crude."

"That's okay, I like crude. And you both are spectacular."

"So are you. I like the sequined sport coat."

"Wait until you see Miss Elva. I think we're going to be the talk of the party when we all enter together."

I followed Beau into the main room while Luna made her call to Mathias. Stopping dead in my tracks, I started laughing.

"Child, I know you aren't laughing at me."

"I am, but in a good way. You're miraculous."

"Of course I am," Miss Elva said, tossing her hair. She was a vision in a dripping caftan in shimmery gold, with a stunning set of fringy sequined butterfly wings attached to her back in black and gold. It should have looked insane. Instead it looked *avant garde*.

"I've never seen anything like it," I said, circling her. The dress clung to her every curve and yet shifted and moved as she walked, and the wings seemed to flutter of their own accord as the fringe moved and danced.

"You think David will like it?"

It wasn't like Miss Elva to be unsure of herself, and I wondered just how much she liked the Flamingo King.

"I think he'll love it."

"I love it. You're a vision, my lovemountain," Rafe

said, hovering over her, his face tinged with sadness. I knew he was working really hard on accepting that he had to share Miss Elva with other men. He was showing remarkable restraint, which surprised me. Who would have thought the pirate ghost could exhibit personal growth?

"Pictures," Irene insisted as Luna came to join the four of us. Taking her phone, Irene snapped a series of us in our finery, smiling brightly at the camera, dripping in sequins and shimmer in the middle of our own private villa.

Looking at the picture, my stomach turned. I couldn't help but feel like this was the calm before the storm.

Luna caught my look. "What's up?"

"Be on guard tonight," I said, "Something's off. I feel it."

"Child, you got your gris-gris on you?"

"Tucked in my shoe," I admitted.

"Good," Miss Elva said and then looked at us. "If Althea says something's up, then something's up. I know we want to party tonight, but how about we not drink for a bit? Get the lay of the land? Keep our wits about us."

"I have no problem with that," Beau said. "I trust you."

"I think we should have a check-in point. It's going to be a massive party, and we might lose each other."

Miss Elva eyed me balefully.

"Well, you'll be hard to lose. But you know what I mean."

"We check in every hour on the hour? At the food tent. If I can't have drinks, I want snacks," Miss Elva decided.

"What are we looking out for?" Beau asked.

"I don't know. Keep an eye on Randall and Calvin. Something's up with those two."

"Got it. I'll see if I can pull any more information from the delightful Captain Woodley."

"Do that. The rest of you, just – you know, do what you do best." I shrugged. As motivational speeches went, it wasn't my finest.

"I do everything my best," Miss Elva preened.

She wasn't wrong.

Chapter Twenty-Nine

THE FLAMINGO KING did not disappoint.

First of all, the man strode up in a bedazzled rhine-stoned flamingo suitcoat, complete with a rhinestone hat and a cape. All he needed was a walking stick and he'd look like a 1970s pimp. Miss Elva all but swooned and Rafe, despite his attempts at being more mature, disappeared in a snit.

"Elva, you are a vision. Will you be my date tonight?" David asked.

I hid a smile at the nervousness in his face. Even if he had a little weight on him, and his tan was just a touch too orange, he was still a handsome man, and it seemed he was really into Miss Elva. They made quite the dashing pair, I had to admit, even if you did need sunglasses to look directly at them.

"I'd like nothing more," Miss Elva said, and took David's arm. "Now, introduce me to all your fancy people and I'll make them jealous with my fabulous outfit."

"Then we'll give them your cards, darling, and they'll snap up your creations in an instant."

"That's the plan," Miss Elva said. Then they drifted into the melee, the sea of people seeming to part for them, then swallow them whole.

"Well, team? What say you?" Luna asked.

"I say… the Flamingo King throws a hell of a party," Beau observed.

He wasn't wrong. There were three wide white tents set up, lit up with string lights, disco balls, and all sorts of flashing lights and smoke machines. There were cage dancers, a stage for a Soul Train set up, and another stage where a band was just warming up by taking the bass for a walk.

Yes, I've always wanted to say that.

Waitresses rolled by on roller-skates, shaking their sequined bottoms to the music. There were more sequins than I think I'd ever seen in my life. Nobody had held anything back – it was one massive party of famous people trying to outdo each other. As this was one of my first major galas with famous people, I had to wonder if this was just how all parties were for them. Were their lives just constant competitions, trying to one-up each other? It sounded exhausting to me.

"I'm kind of dying for those roller-skates. Did you see they have rhinestones on them?" Beau whispered in my ear.

"You could open a drive-in restaurant. You know, where the waiters roll up to you on roller-skates and you eat in your car?"

"That's not a bad idea," Beau mused.

"Where would it be?" Luna asked.

"There's that lot for sale by the highway. It'd be perfect for people looking for a fun place to stop to eat on the way to Key West, without having to go too far off the road."

"What would I call it?" Beau asked.

"Roll On Out?"

"Keep It Rollin'?" Luna offered.

"Rock & Roll?"

"That's How We Roll," I decided, and Beau crowed in delight.

"Want to go in with me?" Beau looked from Luna to me.

"Us? In the restaurant biz?" I looked at Luna and she shrugged a delicate shoulder.

"Could we do a drive-in movie too?"

"Roll the Tape?" I offered, and Beau laughed again.

"I suspect we can make a lot of puns."

"I'm in."

"Me too."

"Welcome to business, partners. Now, let's go find the food. Because you know, that's how we roll," Beau said, testing it out.

I groaned. "That's gonna get old."

"Not as old as those tired maxi-dresses you wear."

"Oh, bitchy," I said, poking him in the ribs.

"Sorry, mama wants a cocktail," Beau apologized.

"It's okay. I'll take some time to revamp my wardrobe. Promise."

"Good. Now, where's the fine man of yours?"

"Cash? I don't know, I haven't seen him yet." A low dredge of worry trickled through my stomach, but I shook it aside. After all, the man could take care of himself.

"I see food. And Captain Woodley," Beau said, veering off with a little wave.

"I'm going to talk to Mama Jean," Luna said, pointing to where Mama Jean was standing. She had poured herself into a mermaid gown, complete with faux sparkle breast covers. I had to pause for a moment just to let the sheer impact of Mama Jean hit me, before I smiled.

"She really turned herself out tonight."

"I would expect nothing less. I think Miss Elva's found her long-lost sister."

"Isn't that the truth? Okay, I'll be back around. I'm just going to circle and see if I can find Cash."

"See you on the hour, remember?" Luna tapped a slim silver watch at her wrist.

"Yup, I remember. Plus, you know, I'm hungry."

"You're always hungry."

"It's part of my charm."

I strolled the perimeter of the party, keeping my eyes out for Cash, but also doing my best to catalog all the celebrities and their outfits. There was a strict no-cell-phone rule at the party, so we'd all left ours at home. But walking through the gala? Gah! I itched for my phone to take photographs. It was like all my celebrity gossip magazines had exploded at once in front of me in real time.

One famous actress, whom I knew for a fact had been featured on the arm of another famous actor in last week's magazine, was canoodling with someone else. Another, who I was certain I'd read had just had a nose job, sucked down champagne like it was water. In the corner, the skinny Adam Levine-style man was talking too fast to a crowd around him and they all laughed politely, though I sensed it was more because he was famous than that he actually had something funny to say. And was that Heidi Klum in a green disco-ball dress? I craned my head to look. I loved her on that designer television show.

Now, I did love my celebrity gossip mags, but when it came to reality television shows, some of my favorites were the ones where people had to design something or cook a meal. It was interesting to me to see how people performed under pressure, and I always enjoyed when they nailed it and delivered a showstopper. I loved seeing people win, so it made me feel good to cheer people on.

Still, I couldn't find Cash. I paused as Calvin approached me, his smile beaming across his face. He looked smashing tonight in a simple black tuxedo, the only nod to the seventies being a sequined bowtie and pocket square.

"Miss Althea, you do not disappoint."

"Thank you, Calvin. Have you seen Cash? I was just trying to find him."

"I haven't, but I'll let him know you are looking for him."

"Thank you. I'll likely be hanging around the food tent. Tell him he can find me there," I said, noticing Randall hovering in the corner, watching us. He smiled when he saw me looking and nodded at me. The smile didn't reach his eyes. I wondered just how much he actually enjoyed putting on these galas, or if he just put up with it for his father.

"I most certainly will. You have some fun tonight, Miss Althea. It's bound to be some party."

"Sure looks that way," I said and stepped away, stopping dead in my tracks a few feet later. Rafe had flown up into my face in a panic.

"I know where the cave is. I found it. I found it, Althea. You have to come."

"Rafe, I can't come right now," I whispered out of the side of my mouth, continuing to walk forward so I didn't look like the crazy person talking to herself.

"No, it has to be now. The tide's coming in. You have to come," Rafe insisted.

"Rafe, there's no way I can go into a cave like this."

"Cash didn't have a problem going in," Rafe said, and I stopped dead in my tracks.

"What did you say?"

"Cash. He went to the cave. I'm not sure I can trust him yet, though. He might steal my treasure. You have to go. Now. The tide is rising."

I looked around, but couldn't see any of my people. Dread began to fill my stomach. If Cash had gone into the cave, and hadn't been seen since...

Oh shit, I was going to have to go.

"Take me," I whispered to Rafe, "But it has to look subtle. Walk me the long way."

"Follow me," Rafe called.

I wandered past Calvin, who paused when he saw me headed away from the food tent.

"Everything all right, Miss Althea?"

"Yup, just stopping back at my villa. I have a bit of indigestion," I said, rubbing my stomach. Calvin grimaced. There was one sure way to get rid of a man, I thought, and that was to talk about having to use the bathroom. Or period cramps. Interchange them as needed.

Without another word, I followed Rafe toward the villa, my heart thumping in my chest as I began to worry about what Rafe had said. If Cash was still in the cave, and the tide was rising – it was only a matter of time.

Picking up my pace, I hurried as fast as my dress would allow. To anyone looking, it would seem like I was making a beeline for my villa. I hoped that supported my indigestion story. Clambering up the steps, I ran inside the villa.

"What are you doing in here? This way," Rafe hissed.

"I had to make it look like I was coming in here. Now, let's go," I said and sailed out the back door, around the pool, and crept down the side of the villa.

"Smart," Rafe admitted. "Now, hurry."

"I'm trying. Just remember I can't fly like you can."

"Oh, right."

Chapter Thirty

I FOLLOWED Rafe the best I could in the dark, my thoughts all on Cash and whether he was in trouble. If he'd fallen and hit his head in the cave, he could drown the instant the water closed in. Running through a gazillion scenarios in my head, I picked up my pace.

Rafe turned at the single palm tree, and I slowed, picking my way down the dirt path. Luckily, Luna had decided to go with a flat strappy sandal, so I wasn't having as much trouble as if I'd been wearing heels. If only the moon were fuller, I'd have better light, I thought, then grunted as I stubbed my toe on a rock.

"Here," Rafe said, coming to a stop and nodding down into the dark hole that yawned before me in the ground.

Now, did I want to go in there? Nope, I most certainly did not. I'd been there before, remember? Things slithered around in there. There was pirate writing on the wall that explicitly warned a person from entering.

"Maybe I should go back and get Luna and Beau," I said. Hindsight and all that. But still. I stared at the dark hole for a while, contemplating what to do, my breath coming in small hitches.

"Cash?" I whispered, hoping he would respond if he heard me. Nothing. Granted, I'd barely whispered it. Leaning lower and cupping my hands around my mouth, I called louder this time. "Cash?"

"Althea!" His voice echoed from far away, "Don't come –"

"Too late," said a voice from behind me, and with one violent shove I was tossed like a ragdoll into the hole. I put my hands out to protect my face and then rolled into a ball as I banged my way down the embankment, coming to a stop at the rock wall where I'd found myself just the night before. "She'll be joining you shortly, lover boy." A light shined in my face, blinding me, but I knew the voice.

"Randall."

"That's right, Miss Psychic. Not so great, are you, if you couldn't foretell this," Randall said, clambering down the hill and wrenching me up, easily flipping me over onto my stomach in the dirt. Realizing he was about to harm me, or restrain me, adrenaline coursed through me. I kicked backwards, hoping to catch his balls, but only just grazing his thigh. A knee came down hard on my back, pressing my face into the dirt, and I whimpered as he cuffed my hands behind me. Once I was restrained, Randall eased off of me. Grabbing me by the cuffs, he pulled me up and shined the light into the cave.

"Walk," he ordered.

"Why?" I asked, stubbornly staying put. Then I let out a yelp as he punched me in the back, doubling over and stumbling forward despite myself. I don't know why it shocked me so much – maybe because I wasn't used to being attacked, or perhaps because I didn't expect it from someone impeccably dressed in a tuxedo. Either way, my lower back screamed in pain, and I blinked back the tears that threatened, doing my best to pay attention to my surroundings as the light flashed on the cavern.

"Forward," Randall ordered, and I went forward, not knowing what else to do, but desperately needing to see what condition Cash was in. The cave, a narrow tunnel in some parts, opened to various rooms and caverns as the path twisted and turned; it felt like we kept going deeper and deeper into the ground. At points there were small ladders to climb down to get to the next level, and for those Randall just dragged me over the edge, not caring if I fell or hurt myself. I felt my ankle go again, knowing that this time it was well and truly twisted, but kept limping along. I tried to memorize what turns we took. Stalactites hung from the ceiling, moisture dripping from them, and the occasional bat whizzed past us, startled by the light. By the time we'd reached the room that Cash was in, I was bloodied, limping, and mad as hell.

"Cash," I gasped as the light shone over him. His face was bruised and bloody, his arms manacled to the wall behind him, and he sat, half-submerged in water, his face mutinous. At least he was conscious, I thought.

"Althea, no," Cash said, his face distraught. He wrenched against the chains that held his wrists.

"Don't bother, lover boy. They aren't going to budge." Randall laughed and tossed me like a sack of potatoes, so that I landed half on Cash. I scrambled away from the water, my sandals slipping on the wet rock, and pushed myself back against the wall next to Cash.

"I'm so sorry, Althea," Cash whispered.

"Why are you sorry? This isn't your fault," I said, nodding at Randall. "It's his."

"Well, now, let's not be so quick to cast blame." Randall laughed, long and high, reminding me a little of the Joker in *Batman*, in his fancy suit and hair that now stood in odd little spikes and tufts around his head. "Although, I suppose it is kind of my fault. Okay, sure, I'll take the blame. Why not? You won't be around to say anything anyway."

"What are you doing?" I asked, watching as he pulled a square of pink from his bag and then began to fill it from a small scuba-like tank. My mouth dropped open as an inflatable flamingo blew up in his lap.

"This, my love, is just some carbon monoxide. I'll

fill this beauty up and then stick a pin in it. Once I close off the entrance, it shouldn't be long until you expire. As deaths go, I think you should thank me. It's quite painless."

The two dead men. The deflated flamingo. It all made sense now.

"The men in the car in Tequila Key. That was your work."

"Indeed. Those assholes were informants. They passed off my flamingo to a second buyer."

"I... I don't understand. Is a flamingo statue really worth killing over?"

Randall threw back his head and laughed, then looked over at me, shaking his head sadly.

"She's pretty, but not very bright, is she?" Randall's face was all edges and craters in the light of the flashlight.

"Sometimes her street smarts are lacking, but that's because she likes to see the best in people."

"Well, my dear, let me tell you a little story then." Randall settled back on his heels and I kept an eye on the canister he'd attached to the flamingo. If the nozzle came out and was still spraying, we'd all be dead pretty shortly. Even with the air flow in this cave, I didn't want to play around with carbon monoxide.

"The flamingo had drugs in it," Cash guessed.

Randall clapped his hands together, like a teacher delighted with his student.

"Yes, yes indeed. A lot of drugs. A lot of very valuable and expensive drugs."

"Is that your thing then? You're a druggie?" I asked.

"No! No, I most certainly am not. The best drug dealers never sample their own stock. No, I am a distributor. One of the best. It's a great spot, this island. One of the last stops before we hit the States. A lot of planes fly through here."

"The plane. Last night."

"Right, exactly. The plane last night was unplanned; they were diverted because of a storm. I would normally never have one land with this many people around. But some things can't be helped. For the most part, people were passed out or smart enough to mind their own business last night. Except you."

"You knew I was here last night."

"You weren't exactly subtle in stumbling your way through the bush in your pajamas. I almost started laughing out loud when you finally realized you were in danger and tried to scuttle out of here. What were you even doing?"

"A crab walk," I said, a defensive note in my voice. I thought I'd been smooth.

"A crab walk. Jesus. You should've just run. Ah, well, it can't be helped."

"Why did you kill the men? And why the flamingo?"

"Because they were delivering my very expensive

cargo to the wrong people and taking the money for it. And I wanted to frame David."

I noticed he said 'David,' and not 'my father.' Inching closer to Cash, I leaned into him, trying to warm him with my body. I had no idea how many hours he'd sat down here in the damp and cold.

"Why? He seems like a nice guy. He's given you a good life. What's the problem?" I asked, and watched the storm cross Randall's face.

"What's the problem? He divorced my mother. Left her a laughingstock at the country club. She could never show her face there again. She was broken after him. And then all of a sudden he becomes the Flamingo King? Further embarrassing her? *Us?* The world looks at us like we're one big joke."

"I don't see that to be true. We all like your dad. He's really nice," I said, my voice soft as I watched the emotions whirl on Randall's face.

"Nice? Nice gets you nowhere. That whole story of him being lonely? Bullshit. He had his wife. Me. A respectable job. How could he be lonely?"

"Because he wasn't happy at his job. It didn't sound like those people were really his friends," Cash offered.

"And your mom was banging the country club pool boy, so I'm pretty sure she's the one everybody's laughing at." Rage flashed across Randall's face and he jumped up, stomping over to me. Whoops, I thought, I really needed to work on that filter.

Randall slapped me across the face, and I cried out

from the shock of it, once again surprised at the violence from this man.

"Don't you talk about my mother like that. She is an angel."

I tasted blood in my mouth, so all I could do was nod.

"She might have made a mistake with the pool boy, but David didn't need to leave her. She was willing to work it out. But he refused. He turned his back on her. What ever happened to vows? He'd vowed to stand by her side when he married her. She broke after he left. It was never the same. She had to get a job, and there was never enough money. She took it out on me, saying it was my fault. That he wouldn't have left if it wasn't for me." Randall's voice cracked.

"But you were just a child," I said, my voice soft, realizing how close this man was to going all the way over the edge. "It wasn't your fault. It wasn't your father's fault either. Your mother made her own choices as an adult. She shouldn't have taken that out on you. You didn't deserve that."

"You don't know what I deserve," Randall shouted at me, and then his lip quivered, like a child about to cry. "I was a naughty boy."

"Randall," I whispered, "You can make this right. We'll help you. You don't have to do this."

"No. No, no, no, no!" Randall clamped his hands on his ears and shook his head back and forth, his screams escalating. I moved closer to Cash so I was pressed completely against his body.

"It's my father's fault. And he's going down for this. They ignored my last flamingo note card, but they can't ignore this one," Randall said. With that he danced his way across the room. Pulling out what looked to be a pin – it was hard to tell in the low light – he slid it into the inflatable flamingo and then tossed the floatie on the rising pool of water. Taking the light up, he shined it on the harbinger of our deaths.

A silly grinning pink flamingo was going to kill us both.

Closing my eyes, I tried to breathe shallowly as Randall scrambled up the ladder from the hole in the cavern. It didn't surprise me in the slightest to hear him laughing maniacally as he shoveled boulders into the opening, sealing Cash and me into our tomb.

As darkness enclosed us, I prayed that Rafe would get help in time.

Chapter Thirty-One

"ALTHEA," Cash whispered, his voice absolutely sounding like defeat.

"Shh, don't say anything. I have to think," I hissed.

"It's… I don't think… the gas will work quickly," Cash said.

"Did I not just tell you to shut up? Let me think," I said. Standing, I hobbled back and forth, antsy and agitated, chasing down a thought I'd had.

"Rafe said there was a tunnel under the water. That we could get out."

"I'm kind of stuck to the wall."

"But if I could get the floatie under the water?"

"And risk popping it in your face?"

"I mean magickally."

"I have no idea how to respond to that."

"Good, best you stay quiet. I need to focus anyway."

Luna had made me learn a moving spell for a

reason. I had two choices: Try and move a massive bolder that sealed us into the cavern, then move the flamingo floatie out into the next cavern; or try to pull the floatie through the water and out to sea. I wasn't confident enough in my science to know how much open-air space we had in this cavern or the next; the carbon monoxide might still do us in. The sea it was.

"Althea –"

"If you say one more word, I'm going to dropkick you just to shut you up."

Cash wisely remained silent.

Channeling myself, and knowing that I had no way to form a circle, I realized I was kind of already wearing one. Pressing my chin down, I felt my quartz necklace still around my neck, and envisioned my power funneling through the crystals. Closing my eyes, I ran the spell through in my head and then envisioned what I wanted to happen, seeing it happening in my mind several times before I was ready to do it. I swallowed against the lump in my throat, and though my voice may have trembled, I incanted the words loudly to the chamber.

"I see the object that I choose,
And I ask the flamingo to move.
I direct it as I see,
As I will, so mote it be."

There was a violent sucking sound, a huge splash of water, and it felt like half the cave got sucked along with the force of my spell, all pulling down, down, down, toward the sea. I leaned into Cash, focusing on envisioning the flamingo until it was out of the cave, and out into the sea. The force of the suction caused the boulders blocking the opening to tumble a bit, and I gasped as I felt fresh air waft over my face.

"What the hell just happened?" Cash asked.

"I... I think I was able to move the flamingo out to sea." I hope so at least, I thought, since I still couldn't see anything.

"Is it possible you could move the bolt of these manacles? If I could just move my arms a bit, I could break the chain."

"Let's give it a go," I said.

I repeated my spell, this time channeling the bolt to break from the wall. I heard chains clinking, then I screeched when a light flashed, blinding me with its sudden brightness.

"Sorry," Cash said, holding up his hand to show me the shark tooth keychain I'd given him.

"My keychain," I said.

"Indeed. Comes in handy," Cash said. He stood, looking around the room. The flamingo was gone, and I hoped we were out of danger.

Finding a rock, Cash came back over to me and motioned for me to turn around.

"I'm going to break the chain between the cuffs."

"Can you do that?"

"These don't look like police-issue cuffs; I think we'll be okay. Hold still," Cash said, and I winced as the stone smashed against the cuffs. But he was right, and in moments I had both hands free, albeit with cuffs on. I looked at Cash, then collapsed in his arms.

"That was really scary," I admitted, loving the feel of his arms around me.

"I know, Althea. But... god, you're just amazing. Did you know you glow when you use your power? You looked like an enchanted mermaid goddess. I've never seen anything like it."

"I didn't know," I admitted.

"We aren't safe here," Cash said, pulling me back. "Let me look at the exit."

Cash strode across the cavern, taking the light with him. A glint in the corner caught my eye and I went to investigate.

"The boulders have moved, but there isn't enough space for us to get through," Cash said. "I worry if I push one, the others will crash down on our heads."

"I could try my moving spell again?"

"That might be the only thing we can do."

"Is that voices I hear down there? You two should be dead by now," Randall laughed from above. "Oh well, I guess I'll need to use another canister."

Cash raced to my side. I scooped up what I'd found on the floor and we looked at each other.

"In the water," I gasped, pulling my dress over my head.

"What? We can't."

"We can. We have to. Give me the light and hold

onto my leg," Thank god I was a strong swimmer and wasn't claustrophobic. I had Trace to thank for that – he'd taken me on many a swim-through tunnel on our dives. This time was a lot different, as we'd only be on one breath of air.

"Can you do this?"

"We have no choice," I said, just as Randall tossed something into the chamber. We took one breath and dove.

Chapter Thirty-Two

LIGHT OR NO LIGHT, it was almost impossible to see because we kicked up so much sediment diving into the water. Feeling with one hand, I found the opening on the other side of the cavern and I pulled us to the surface.

"One more big breath," I ordered. Cash nodded and we both took a deep breath before I pulled him under and held the little keychain light in front of me, kicking as hard as I could through the tunnel. I prayed it wasn't so long that Cash and I would end up fish food.

Together we swam until the little light in the keychain sputtered out, the water finally having gotten to the electronics, and still we kicked along. Finally I felt the ceiling of the tunnel give way above my head. Kicking upwards, I almost cried when my head broke the surface.

"Where are we?" Cash asked, turning, and for a

moment, all we could see was darkness. As my eyes adjusted, I finally saw just a hint of ambient light coming from the tunnel in the corner of the room.

"I think this is the cavern we swam into the other day – where you kissed me. If so, we should be able to swim right out – no need for dive tanks."

"Let's go," Cash said. I wondered how he could swim with the chains still on his wrist and whatever other injuries he had sustained. There was no time to ask, though – we both swam for our lives through the tunnel, then out into the dark water where the sliver of moon seemed to be the brightest light ever. I could have laughed if I wasn't so terrified.

Something brushed my leg and I kicked out.

"Cash, we need to get on land. Soon," I said.

"Althea… I think –"

I heard the slap of a paddle against the water just as he did and was shocked to see a man on a paddle board in the water.

"Um."

"It's me. Get on," Calvin ordered.

I froze. Why was he out here? Was he in on it with Randall? But when I felt another bump against my leg, I made my choice. It was either get on that paddle board with Calvin, or stay and try to make nice with the sharks.

Now, I loved sharks and usually loved diving with them. But I was currently in distress, and they could read those signals very clearly. I took my chances and climbed on the board with Calvin. Cash followed me and put his arms around me.

"Be very quiet," Calvin warned.

Neither of us said anything as he gently paddled us closer to shore. I knew that Cash was tensing, ready to spring and take him down if needed.

Above on the cliff, a shadow of a man emerged. I knew it was Randall from the way he raged, his hair in spikes, his arms thrown to the air. Turning, he looked down at the water and I knew in that instant that he could see us clear as day on the water. He reached into his pocket, pulled out a gun, and drew on us.

I screamed as a shot was fired, and then gasped as the paddle board hit the sand. Randall jerked backward and then forward, toppling headfirst over the cliff and into the water. Silence greeted us as we all held our breath.

"Calvin, you saved us." I looked up at Calvin, who smoothly pocketed his gun and then held out his hand to me.

"Dat man, he not right in de head. I worried 'bout him."

"How'd you know to be out here?"

"I followed him. No way I could get in de cave after you, but I hoped you'd remember de way out. It's why I took you to dis beach. Just in case."

"You could've warned us," Cash said, while unbuttoning his soaking shirt and handing it to me to pull around myself.

"Nothing to warn about," Calvin shrugged. "I just had my suspicions."

"You saw me go into the cave."

"I did. But I couldn't follow once I realized he was playing with de gas. I be no help to you if I be passed out."

"Thank you," I said, surprising him with a hug.

"Dat's no problem, Miss Althea. I have a daughter around your age. She'd want me to do de same for her."

"What will we tell the Flamingo King"

"We can tell him de truth, or we tell him Randall drank too much and drowned. I don't know which will be easier on him."

"Is it easier to mourn if he knows his son hated him all along?" Cash asked.

"I tink dat may break his heart even more. I don't know de right answer."

"He killed other people. And there's a drug ring," I pointed out.

"Yes, I tink de truth is always de best then."

"That it is," I agreed.

We all reached the top of the cliff to find the rest of our entourage gaping at us. The Flamingo King strode forward.

"What's going on here? Is everyone okay?"

"David, I'm sorry, but you'll need to call de police,"

Calvin said, and went forward, putting his arm around David's shoulders. I saw the Flamingo King jerk in shock, and I wished I could spare him the pain he was feeling.

"It was Randall, wasn't it?" Miss Elva asked, and I nodded to her, my eyes full of sorrow.

"I'll take care of him. You both okay?"

"We are. You go with David. He needs somebody right now," I said, and Miss Elva went. Her wings fluttered behind her like an angel now as she pulled a sobbing David into her arms.

"Althea, what happened? Why are you in Cash's shirt?"

"Couldn't swim in the dress," I said.

"Nice boobs," Rafe leered.

"Hey, you took your sweet time getting help." I glared at him, crossing my arms over my chest.

"Nobody was listening to me!" Rafe's eyes sharpened. "What's in your hand?"

"Oh, just a little something I found in the cave."

Even in the wan light of the moon the stones glistened. A chunky gemstone necklace dripping in diamonds led to a fat sapphire center stone, surrounded by even more diamonds.

"You found it!" Rafe breathed.

"I did. And I don't know what I'll do with it yet. Right now I'd like to get some clothes on."

"Why bother? You look great with them off."

"You know what, Rafe? I think that's the nicest thing you've ever said to me."

"I think he's just trying to get his necklace back," Rosita said.

"Little shit."

Epilogue

"YOU KNOW I invest in things, right? It's kind of what I do," Cash said, crossing his tanned legs and leaning over to steal a sip of my rum punch.

"I might have heard that a time or two," I agreed, pulling my sunglasses from my hair and sliding them over my eyes, a smile playing on my lips.

"And I happen to think 'That's How We Roll' is a great name," he said, finishing my drink.

"Hey!" I exclaimed. "That was mine."

"Unlimited drinks, remember?"

We were comfortably ensconced at the Flamingo King's guest villa, and the staff had been told to see to our every need. Beau and Luna, after making sure we were unharmed and able to function, had flown home earlier that day with Captain Woodley at the helm of the plane. Cash and I had been asked – well, more like instructed – by the local police force to stay put, and the Flamingo King had graciously offered to extend our stay. Not only did he not hold his son's death against us, but he was visibly traumatized about the danger Randall had put us in. Beneath all the fluff and feathers, it seemed the Flamingo King was truly a nice man, and he was devastated to know his son had hurt people.

David's usual exuberance had dimmed, like someone had flicked off the light switch, and Miss Elva had gone into full protection mode. She'd already informed me that she planned to stay here awhile, just until she could coax the King back into some semblance of his former self. In the meantime, it was me and Luna to check on her house and make sure the more esoteric needs of the Tequila Key community were met.

A staff member materialized at our side and we ordered another round of drinks, relaxing back onto our lounge chairs.

"I don't think I could get used to this," I admitted, even though I was enjoying every moment of this luxury.

"Really? Why's that?"

"I think I'd get bored. I like working," I said, turning to look at Cash. "No wonder the really rich are always buying new things or traveling all the time. I think without creative projects or work, life has to get pretty bland."

"Only you would sit out by this beautiful pool and call it bland," Cash laughed.

"I'm serious though, I think I always want to work. Or create. It's good for your soul."

"I can see that. I could retire on my investments alone right now, but there's no way I'd do that."

"You want more, more, more?"

"Nah, I have enough. But I like the thrill of the hunt. I like finding new projects, investing in people's futures, and seeing their dreams pay off. Much like your new drive-in idea."

"Still nope. No outside investors," I said, smiling my thanks at the staff member who brought us fresh drinks – margaritas this time.

"Hey! I'm not really an outsider, am I?"

"Not to me, you're not. But in Tequila Key? Yes. You need to have been there a minimum of ten to fifteen years before you're on the inside."

"I guess I have my work cut out for me. How about I consult?"

"Maybe." I pushed a curl out of my face. "What's the fee?"

"Time with you?"

"Hmmm, trading sex for consulting sounds a lot like prostitution," I chided, and a deep smile slashed Cash's handsome face.

"Who said anything about sex?"

"Damn it," I exclaimed.

Cash threw back his head and laughed. "Something on your mind, Althea?"

"Nope." I got up and jumped in the pool, not caring

if I splashed, but needing the cool water to relax me. Cash dove in right after me and came up behind me, circling my waist with his arms. Holding me against him for a moment, he kissed my head.

"I'm glad you're not too hurt."

"My ankle will take a while. Luna will work on it when I get home. I'm glad you're not too banged up either."

"Mainly bruises and swelling. It'll all heal."

"I was scared." I blew out a breath.

"Yeah, me too. Let's not do that again."

"Cash, my life is… complicated." I turned and looked up at him. "I don't know what I can promise you right now. I don't know where things will go. And I can't even promise you that I won't end up in another situation like the one today. I'm kind of a mess."

"Good thing I like cleaning up messes," Cash said, bending to brush his lips over mine.

"Are you willing to take things as they come right now? I'm…" I held a hand to my stomach. "Everything's all tangled up and weird down here."

"If you promise to always be honest with me, then yes, I'll take things as they come."

"It's a deal. I may be a mess, but I'm not a liar."

"Then we take it a day at a time. And you know what I want to do on this day?"

"What's that?"

"Hmm, I'd better just show you," Cash said.

I gasped with laughter as he lifted me over his

shoulder like a sack of potatoes and walked around the side of the pool. I had a feeling I knew just where he was taking me, and heat tugged low in my belly.

But instead, he tossed me right back into the pool. The last thing I saw before I went under was him laughing as though he was the funniest guy in the world.

Oh yeah, I'd show him.

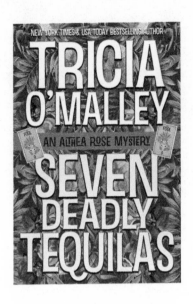

Available from Amazon

The following is a sneak peak from
Seven Deadly Tequilas
Book 7 in the Althea Rose Mystery Series

Chapter One

I CLAPPED MY HANDS, making the blonde-haired Real Housewife of Tequila Key jump in her seat and blink at me balefully from beneath lashes coated heavily in mascara. Keeping Missy Sue on track was like wrangling a pile of puppies and while I usually managed her well enough, today was trying my patience.

"Missy Sue! What is on your mind today? You're barely paying attention." I admonished my monthly client softly and pushed the tarot deck toward her once again. "What are we focusing this reading on?"

Ever since Luna and I had been featured – not to our particular joy, mind you, in several of the gossip magazines – Missy Sue had shown up faithfully each month with ever-increasing wild questions for the tarot cards. First, she'd come to try and contact her father who had recently passed. After that, she'd come back each month to ask more questions about her father. As far as I was concerned, a client could get a reading as many times as their credit card allowed, but in all reality, it was my belief that the tarot cards didn't like to be asked the same questions over and over. When I'd gently mentioned that fact to Missy Sue, she'd started bringing different questions to the table, each one more extravagant than the next, and I suspected she enjoyed telling her "Ladies who Lunch" crowd about her monthly meetings with her celebrity psychic.

Not that it mattered much to me – any advertising was good advertising. I could say that with a straight face now that my bikini-clad butt wasn't plastered across the gossip magazines and my authenticity was no longer being called into question. Well, no more than usual that is. There's something about psychics that just bring out the worst skeptics in people. I was used to my skills being put under a magnifying glass – just not typically on a national scale.

"Um, do you think Sheena is going to divorce Bryson?" Missy Sue picked up the cards and I rolled my eyes, stopping her.

"We've talked about this, Missy Sue."

"Oh, right. I have to ask questions about my own life."

"Yes, you're meant to do a reading for you. You can't use tarot to get the gossip on other people in town."

"Fine." Missy Sue sighed, winding a strand of blonde hair around her finger, nails tipped in coral pink, and then brightened. "Okay, got it. Will my father's grave get robbed?"

Well, *that* was certainly a new one. Blowing out a breath, I counted to three and then looked over at my skeleton, Herman, sporting a Pink Floyd t-shirt today, and wondered if I should just cancel Missy Sue's appointment. She was clearly not focused today, and my patience was wearing thin. Not like I'd ever been thick on patience, and wasn't that a weird thought? Trying to visualize what the thickness and thinness of patience would look like, I pulled myself back and refocused on Missy Sue who was looking at me expectantly. *Now* who was the one not focused?

"Missy Sue…what on earth are you talking about?"

"You know, because of the grave robber in town?" Missy Sue leaned over, her pretty face lighting up as much as it could under the layers of Botox, and she lowered her voice to a hush. "You haven't heard?"

"No, I haven't heard."

"I'm shocked. I thought scary stuff like that would come right to you. Since you're into death and all that…" Missy Sue gave Herman a look.

"I'm not into death, Missy Sue. I simply understand there are spirits among us and know that our reality is not all that we see."

"Is there one here now?" Missy Sue looked wildly around.

"One what?" I asked, my mind on the grave robber.

"A spirit?

"Oh," I looked around and saw Rosita, a ghostly Madam, waft through the screen that separated my area from Luna's shop. "Yup, sure is."

"There is? Where?" Missy Sue's eyes widened to the size of saucers and a light sheen of sweat broke out on her upper lip.

"Missy Sue. It's fine. Spirits exist around us. They don't want to hurt us. Now, your time is running short... anything else you'd like to ask?" I nudged the cards again. Missy Sue shot to her feet when a book from my shelf tumbled off and it took everything in my power not to yell at a grinning Rosita.

"Was that a ghost?"

"Nope, just cheap shelves." I lied and shot a quick glare at Rosita who made a very unladylike gesture back in my direction.

"Uh, well, so...I started selling a new line of all-natural cleaning products. Do see me being successful?" Missy Sue finally focused, shuffling the cards dutifully, while darting quick glances over her shoulder at the book that had landed on the ground next to her.

"That's a great question to ask," I said, watching as she cut the cards into three piles. Reaching for the cards, I quickly dealt out a simple Celtic Cross spread and examined the cards while Missy Sue looked on hopefully. The cards, surprisingly, indicated she would be. With an eye on the clock, I ran through the reading quickly and was happy to see the flush of pleasure that crossed Missy Sue's face. As she packed her bag to leave, I stopped her.

"What about this grave robber now?"

"Oh, well, I can't believe you haven't heard! It's all everyone is talking about."

Her everyone and *my* everyone varied greatly, so I wasn't entirely shocked I hadn't heard the news yet.

"I've been busy."

"Well, two graves have been robbed at the cemetery out by the highway now. Right by that godawful sign?"

Years ago, an intrepid mayor had thought to put a sign proclaiming, "Tequila Makes It Better," hoping to draw tourists to our little downtown. Instead, tourists paused for a photo and continued on their way to the party town of Key West.

"Yup, I know the cemetery. So, it's being robbed for…jewelry?"

"No! That's the shocking thing," Missy Sue held a hand to her heart and dropped her voice again, "The bodies have gone missing."

Available from Amazon

Afterword

Thank you for spending time with my book, I hope you enjoyed the story.

Have you read books from my other series? Join our little community by signing up for my newsletter for updates on island-living, giveaways, and how to follow me on social media!
http://eepurl.com/1LAiz.

or at my website
www.triciaomalley.com

Please consider leaving a review! Your review helps others to take a chance on my stories. I really appreciate your help!

Ms. Bitch

FINDING HAPPINESS IS THE BEST REVENGE

New from Tricia O'Malley
Read Today

From the outside, it seems thirty-six-year-old Tess Campbell has it all. A happy marriage, a successful career as a novelist, and an exciting cross-country move ahead. Tess has always played by the rules and it seems like life is good.

Except it's not. Life is a bitch. And suddenly so is Tess.

"Ms. Bitch is sunshine in a book! An uplifting story of fighting your way through heartbreak and making your own version of happily-ever-after."
~Ann Charles, USA Today Bestselling Author of the Deadwood Mystery Series

"Authentic and relatable, Ms. Bitch packs an emotional punch. By the end, I was crying happy tears and ready to pack my bags in search of my best life."
-Annabel Chase, author of the Starry Hollow Witches series

"It's easy to be brave when you have a lot of support in your life, but it takes a special kind of courage to forge a new path when you're alone. Tess is the heroine I hope I'll be if my life ever crumbles down around me. Ms. Bitch is a journey of determination, a study in self-love, and a hope for second chances. I could not put it down!"

-Renee George, USA Today Bestselling Author of the Nora Black Midlife Psychic Mysteries

"I don't know where to start listing all the reasons why you should read this book. It's empowering. It's fierce. It's about loving yourself enough to build the life you want. It was honest, and raw, and real and I just...loved it so much!"

– Sara Wylde, author of Fat

The Mystic Cove Series

Wild Irish Heart

Wild Irish Eyes

Wild Irish Soul

Wild Irish Rebel

Wild Irish Roots: Margaret & Sean

Wild Irish Witch

Wild Irish Grace

Wild Irish Dreamer

Wild Irish Christmas (Novella)

Wild Irish Sage

Available in audio, e-book & paperback!

Available from Amazon

"I have read thousands of books and a fair percentage have been romances. Until I read Wild Irish Heart, I never had a book actually make me believe in love."- Amazon Review

The Isle of Destiny Series

ALSO BY TRICIA O'MALLEY

Stone Song

Sword Song

Spear Song

Sphere Song

Available in audio, e-book & paperback!

Available from Amazon

"Love this series. I will read this multiple times. Keeps you on the edge of your seat. It has action, excitement and romance all in one series."- Amazon Review

The Siren Island Series

ALSO BY TRICIA O'MALLEY

Good Girl

Up to No Good

A Good Chance

Good Moon Rising

Too Good to Be True

Available in audio, e-book & paperback!

Available from Amazon

"Love her books and was excited for a totally new and different one! Once again, she did NOT disappoint! Magical in multiple ways and on multiple levels. Her writing style, while similar to that of Nora Roberts, kicks it up a notch!! I want to visit that island, stay in the B&B and meet the gals who run it! The characters are THAT real!!!" - Amazon Review

Author's Note

Thank you for taking a chance on my books; it means the world to me. Writing novels came by way of a tragedy that turned into something beautiful and larger than itself (see: *The Stolen Dog*). Since that time, I've changed my career, put it all on the line, and followed my heart.

Thank you for taking part in the worlds I have created; I hope you enjoy it.

I would be honored if you left a review online. It helps other readers to take a chance on my work.

As always, you can reach me at
info@triciaomalley.com
or feel free to visit my website at
www.triciaomalley.com.

Author's Acknowledgement

First, and foremost, I'd like to thank my family and friends for their constant support, advice, and ideas. You've all proven to make a difference on my path. And, to my beta readers, I love you for all of your support and fascinating feedback!

And last, but never least, my two constant companions as I struggle through words on my computer each day - Briggs and Blue.

Made in the USA
Las Vegas, NV
12 March 2022

45441246R00163